GOODLIFE, MISSISSIPPI

Praise for *Goodlife, Mississippi* by Eileen Saint Lauren

"*Goodlife, Mississippi*, is a story of a young girl who has an extraordinary capacity for love. Misfortune finds Mary Myra Boone, but, bless her heart, she endures and even manages to rise. Eileen Saint Lauren has created a memorable character who will linger with you long after the final page. *Goodlife, Mississippi*, is an inspirational book of faith set among the rhythms and customs of a not-so-distant Mississippi."

—Lee Martin, author of Pulitzer Prize Finalist
for *The Bright Forever*.

"Eileen Saint Lauren's *Goodlife, Mississippi*, is characterized by brilliance of expression, vivacity, wit, and a rare quality these days, compassion. Saint Lauren is practically the Daughter of Faulkner. I believe that she is in the line with the great Southern writers Faulkner, Welty, Lee, etc."

—Charles Edward Eaton, American Poet,
Novelist, Golden Rose Award.

"Eileen Saint Lauren is an heiress of Eudora Welty—with verve, strangeness, and Mississippi tonality. I have found her fiction, *Goodlife, Mississippi*, spritely, comic, and rather wild in a Southern romantic vein."

—Richard Wilbur, Poet Laurette,
twice Pulitzer Prize winner for
Poetry, Robert Frost Medal.

Goodlife, Mississippi, is a story of a self-made orphan whose guilty conscience and search for her true calling led her to her destiny and the blue sky of Home. Set in the Deep South at a time of segregation, Eileen Saint Lauren, through the eyes of her own heart—as wide as the Mississippi—casts a spell on the reader and offers us the light as seen through all the colors of the rainbow (the hue-man spectrum—culture + humanity) rendering life as a meaningful whole. A celebration both boisterous and haunting, this is a book of revelation and redemption which lifts the spirit and nurtures the soul."

—Antonia Alexandra Klimenko,
Poet in Residence for the SpokenWord Paris,
France, author of *On the Way to Invisible*.

"Eileen Saint Lauren's debut novel *Goodlife, Mississippi*, chronicles the first twelve years of Myra Boone in a first-person narrative deliciously heavy with the suck and smell of Mississippi mud."

—Anna Jean Mayhew, author of
Tomorrow's Bread. Sir Walter Raleigh Award
for Fiction, SIBA Book Award Finalist.

"*Goodlife, Mississippi*, is an eccentric, inspirational story about how one young girl harnesses her gifts in a crazy, poverty-stricken South."

—Margaret McMullan, author of
Where the Angels Lived.

"In *Goodlife, Mississippi*, young Myra Boone may not have a formal education, but she articulates her experiences with loneliness, race, disability, and loss in the Deep South with the grit, compassion, and grace that only come from a lifetime of looking to see and listening to understand. I found it a privilege to walk alongside her as she discovered strength, healing, and purpose in the right—if unexpected—places."

—Maura Weller, author
of the Catholic Press Association
Award-winning *Contrition*.

GOODLIFE, MISSISSIPPI

Eileen Saint Lauren

EILEEN SAINT LAUREN BOOKS
CHAPEL HILL, NC (USA)

EILEEN SAINT LAUREN BOOKS
CHAPEL HILL, NC (USA)

GOODLIFE, MISSISSIPPI

ISBN 979-8-9861963-0-5
1. Southern Gothic—Fiction 2. African American men—Ray Charles Robinson 3. Literature of the American South—Segregation, Mississippi. I. Title

Book design by Arash Jahani

In loving memory of Fenton Van Buren Stringer, Shirley Arabelle Davis Stringer, and Lorena R-Cola Reynolds Davis—my parents and grandma from South Mississippi.

For Him

GOODLIFE, MISSISSIPPI

MYRA

Chapter 1

IN SPRING OF 1961, we were living in Meridian, Mississippi, in a little plank house that Daddy had made and painted white with his own two hands because he was a carpenter and all. He got the wood at the sawmill and from left over carpentering jobs. It had a tin roof that when it rained, you could count the raindrops until you fell sound, sound asleep. It was as fine as you can imagine with not only the usual two bedrooms, but we were blessed enough to have three. Momma was as proud as any North Carolina Cherokee Indian chief who had won out and had been given his own land back sitting on our front porch in her store-bought rocker fanning the Southern heat and believing that the Boone family had been blessed with the joy of the Lord.

I tried to make myself satisfied. That was for sure. But the embarrassing facts remained; my daddy was a deaf drunk who, for all my life, shared a love-hate affair with moonshine whiskey. And to cope with Daddy's drinking infidelity, Momma began her own love affair with the Lord Jesus Christ. There was nothing I could do but watch and pray that we'd all be saved, mainly from each other.

Listening to the voice of Momma's words is how I learned the rhythms of reading and writing. Then, amid my Meridian Piney Woods of solitude and the long hellish days of summer, I took to copying entire books from the Bible, word for word, to keep from going insane amid the Mississippi heat and the isolation that came with living in the Piney Woods. My other means of escape was reading mail-order catalogs that came once a month by way of the United States Post Office postmarked "New York City." I found myself torn been two cities, Heaven and New York, that to me were one and the same, though I never dared speak of the latter.

Like many God-fearing Southerners, rich or poor, black, or white, I was taught to live to die, and *only then* would I have a good life—in heaven not hell, that is.

Death doesn't scare me none, but life sure does. I don't know why

I'm still here.

MARIGOLD DAVIS WAS my momma's given name. She grew up at Magnolia Sunday in Goodlife, Mississippi, where her folks grew cantaloupes, watermelons, and raised hogs. All she ever did with her life in Goodlife was teach children Sunday School at the Union Community Church in the neighboring town of Soso. In Meridian, she took care of her family—us. And though she was told she was of the Jefferson Davis blood line, the day she married my daddy, Virgil Boone, was the last day on God's green earth that her folks ever spoke to her for everyone thought that Daddy would never amount to a hill of beans. After declaring their love and marrying in a private wedding ceremony the good Lord only knows where and shaking the Davis family along with the entire city of Goodlife to their cores, my folks moved to Meridian to get away from the dead silence and careless whispers that surrounded them. But living in Meridian wasn't any better than living in Goodlife.

It didn't help strengthen family relations or build earthly friendships that Daddy ran moonshine whiskey to make ends meet. And it didn't help our reputation that behind our backs everyone called us *n-lovers* and me *white trash* either. For that time in Mississippi history, 1961, anyone who so as much as spoke a single word to a Negro or "Colored," let alone broke bread with one, was instantly doomed and surrounded by white whispers that in the blink of an eye ruined his or her family name.

To make life even harder for me to understand, it was rumored that Daddy had some Negro blood in him, as much as one-tenth, possibly making him of mixed-race. However, it was never confirmed. Now one-tenth doesn't sound like much, but even a drop of Negro blood in the once segregated South was equal to being given a death sentence in the electric chair in the Mississippi State Penitentiary or even worse, strung up by the neck to hang from a tree limb until your feet kicked the life right out of you. Momma said it was because he liked to keep company with the Negros day in and day out. Daddy did bring Coloreds like our best friends, Opal and Eddy, to the house to break bread and eat collard greens often. We even took them places with us. That much I know to be true. Still, I know nothing of the *actual* color of blood that flowed through his veins or mine.

Looking back, it could very well be true though. See, Daddy passed the time off by telling us stories of him and Ray Charles Robinson. He'd tell of riding the roads together back in Saint Augustine, Florida, when they were charity students in a state-supported boys' school for the deaf and blind learning a trade on account of their shortcomings; Daddy was deaf, and Ray was blind.

Ray dropped *Robinson*, so folks wouldn't confuse him with the boxer Sugar Ray Robinson. It was Ray who in-full-force hit the pavement first to Seattle, Washington, before moving on to Hollywood, California. Daddy hit the moonshine whiskey bottle as fast, only to nowhere save for carpentering in Meridian.

I guess I knew about Ray Charles before I knew of any other musical performer. In the 50s and 60s, folks called him *Colored* instead of Negro or Black or African American like folks do today. *Colored* sounds like the racial remark it is, but the once-segregated South has come a long way from saying the *N-word*, that's for sure. I never used that word because I was a God-fearing, church-going Believer who took the words seriously that we sang in the song "Jesus loves the Little Children."

We would sing: Jesus loves the little children / All the children of the world / *Red, brown, and yellow / Black and white / They are precious in His sight. / Jesus loves the little children / Of the world.* So, it didn't matter to me if Ray Charles was Colored or green or what, he was my *hero*. Some folks dreamed of meeting Elvis Presley one day. My dream was to meet Ray Charles. I had another dream too, to be a bonafide writer.

To keep our spirits high, we sang. And sing we did. When I was eleven-years-old my momma sang *You Are My Sunshine* to me right along with Ray Charles on the box radio. Having a song and sunshine in your heart makes life worth living.

MANY YEARS PASSED, eleven almost, twelve to be exact, without Momma seeing her folks, let alone them meeting me because of the consequences that came with the choices she had made in the name of love. Isolation in the Piney Woods had slowly chipped away at the Davis pride she once had in being a Sunday School teacher in Soso. It was the lack of love and the support of a family that had worn the high polish off her golden upbringing at Magnolia Sunday, leaving her with a defeated, tarnished look. That Christmas day in 1950 when I was born, Momma truly believed that *I was* an answer to prayer. She said I was her sunshine. And *I was* all that she had in the world to love and live for. In a sense, Momma said I was like baby Jesus and that I had an earthly mission to fulfill. Otherwise, I'd have died at birth beings as I was a breech baby and all. My mission was to pray for a miracle for Daddy to be healed of his deafness. Only then would all our sadness disappear and could we live a good life. See, when I came along, Momma latched on like a snapping turtle to the hope that came with me. She never let me go anywhere. Not even to school. That made my life hard—then and now.

Some said Daddy couldn't help being deaf. I never knew if that was true or not. Daddy stayed home with us to drink his fill of moonshine whiskey and kept us awake for years. Only on holidays did he take to riding the roads in his truck that I named, The Rainbow. He would surprise everyone he knew with a handful of Hershey Kisses and an oyster jar of his best moonshine whiskey with a big red ribbon tied around its lid. He always hid some liquor in the dirty clothes box in our indoor bathroom. He hid his whiskey still deep in the Meridian Piney Woods. Once a year on his birthday, when he had an extra dollar in his pocket to burn, he'd treat himself to three pints of store-bought vodka and three packs of Pall Mall cigarettes. He said three was his lucky number—him, Momma, and me.

Momma never understood Daddy any more than he understood himself. It wasn't until *after* they married that she learned the truth about his weaknesses. The eyes of her heart opened to Daddy when she saw him at the soda counter of Woolworth's in Hattiesburg, Mississippi, sipping on a Frostie Root Beer float with not one but three brightly colored party straws. He was with four other workers all carpenters and window washers in Hattiesburg when they weren't picking cotton from sunrise to sunset in the fields of Jones County in the Union Community to make ends meet. Momma then worked the vanilla ice cream machine. She'd put square blocks of ice in the top of it along with rock salt then add the necessary eggs, sugar, cream, condensed milk, and vanilla flavoring to make it all sugar sweet. She wore a pink and white pinstriped skirt and blouse and navy shoes with crisp white shoelaces. No socks though. Momma despised anything made of cotton to touch her bare feet. She said socks reminded her of the Coloreds working in the hot Mississippi fields. On Saturdays, she changed her shoelaces to *yellow* because yellow was a happy color.

Beings Sunday was the Lord's Day, she was off. Sunday was also when everyone from Goodlife to Soso to Glossolalia to Goshen either rested or visited the sick and shut-ins, the heathens, the jailbirds, or the mentally retarded folks at the Ellisville State School. Folks were taught to spread any extra love they had in their hearts around to those who needed it. In Mississippi, a lot of people needed love, then and now. People everywhere need love.

At the five-and-dime soda fountain, Daddy paid with dollar bills. Right away Momma was attracted to him. She said it was his laugh that made her take a second look, not George Washington's face laying on top of the soda fountain stool he'd left behind for her as a tip one Saturday. Then, she noticed how his smooth, tanned skin framed his face under his navy company cap that had a shoot of cotton embroidered in its center like a dogwood blossom. Once, he had showed up at Magnolia Sunday along with the other folks in the Union Community who came to listen and dance to the Grand Ole Opry on the box radio in the cool of a Saturday evening. That's when they began to court. They hid behind Magnolia Sunday and danced to the music of the night air.

While Daddy's first smile took him straight to your heart, he was a handsome man as well. He was courteous, generous, and compassionate with everyone who crossed his path beings he had no living family that he knew of. It was told to him that his folks got shed of him on account of his deafness, believing him to be mentally retarded. Folks used to think that if you had a birth defect like deafness, you needed to be institutionalized. A *retard* is what they called Daddy.

Daddy was made fun of and beat down all his life for the way he spoke on account of his deafness. He stuttered bad. And sometimes, he slobbered on himself, especially if he got excited. Yet from my daddy's first smile and *Th-aaa-nk y-ooo-u, k-iii-nd-ly,* his spirit entered Momma's heart. Drunk as a skunk or sober as a preacher man, mean as a Sweetwater, Texas, rattlesnake, happy like a hobo tan-faced clown or white or black or Mulatto, deaf of sound and hearing, no matter what he was, Momma loved him. And I loved him too.

Daddy's overall feeling about himself in society was a total and sure emptiness. I write with certainty because he transferred that empty feeling to me. He never felt like he would be able to dig *himself*, let alone the Boone family, out of the poor house he'd provided for us with carpentering, window-washing, and running moonshine whiskey in The Rainbow. The careless white whispers we endured that he was a *Nobody* and a good-for-nothing drunk added to our sense of emptiness.

As hard as it was for us and as lonely as we often found ourselves, Daddy believed the peace found in the tender grass of one's soul was a miracle for anyone. He told me it didn't matter if a man had a shiny new dime or a crisp green dollar in his pocket. If he had peace in his soul, he was as rich as cream.

Daddy had always felt stuck in the Deep South. The truth is *we were all stuck* in Mississippi. A lot of times folks, rich or poor, who have nowhere else to go or anyone to turn to for comfort will turn to the Lord, the church house, or the power of prayer. Or they fall by the wayside into a pit of sin where their weaknesses win out to Satan, the devil. That's what my folks did in Meridian. Momma fell hard for Jesus Christ and became so religious that I wasn't even allowed to go into the first grade for fear I'd get exposed to sin and become hell-bound. Daddy fell by the wayside into the nothingness that comes after the whiskey bottle is empty.

At the tender age of eleven, I began my journey into the spirit world—a world that can only be seen and moved about in with the eyes of the heart. A world that is never-ending, infinite. A deeper world within the world that we are living in where the supernatural power of God, the devil, and their angels never cease to exist. I heard voices and saw things outside myself that I've never shared with anyone until now.

I grew up surrounded by throwaways, the downtrodden, and the lonely. I loved them and they loved me. I wanted to be connected to someone, something, or somebody by way of *hope* that comes with brotherly unconditional Christian love, but all I saw growing up in the Bible Belt was twisted and conditional love until I began learning the secret things of God that I aim to share with you.

By the way, my given name is Mary Myra Boone, but everyone calls me Myra. This is my story. I hope you will read on.

THE GREETING CARD

Chapter 2

"BABYDOLL, HAVE YOU got your greeting cards handy? Get a yellow one out and fix it up as nice as you can for your Great Aunt Annabelle before we head on out to Happy Acres old folks' home to visit with her. Hear?" Momma asked me, pulling her slip over her head.

"Why in the world do you want a *yellow* one of all things?" I asked on my way to my bedroom to search for the box of greeting cards.

"When Aunt Annabelle was in the Mississippi State Mental Hospital back in 1946, she fell in love with the color yellow because one of the finest doctors in the state, Doc Jasper, brought her a yellow rose from Texas. And since he was the only real doctor who she had ever laid eyes on, and he had rode his mare out to her old home place in Eastern Tennessee nestled in the Great Smoky Mountains, old Doc Jasper impressed her far more than if President Harry Truman had come all the way from Washington, D.C., to personally ask for her vote. It was Doc Jasper who told her anything *yellow* would give her strength. And she believed him like he was preaching the gospel. That's why."

"Why did she go to the Mississippi State Mental Hospital if she was living in the Great Smoky Mountains?" I asked, looking outside to see my cat Kitty Momma on the window ledge silent as snow falling in December, pondering no doubt to what we were getting all fixed up for.

"Her old man, Uncle Andrew Stringer, had dropped dead right in the middle of tending his tobacco fields early one April morning. She didn't have a soul in the world except her baby sister and my momma, your Grandma Reatha, and her husband, Spurgeon Davis, to go live with. She ended up at their home place, Magnolia Sunday, over in Goodlife for a spell, but as soon as she took sick with her mind, they rushed her straight to the Mississippi State Hospital simply because it was the finest in the South." Momma went on to tell me as she walked into the hall all dressed but a hat, "And it still is."

I fumbled through the greeting cards I'd hidden under my bed. Daddy had a birthday just around the corner, and I was afraid he would see his card before time. And I certainly didn't want that to happen. Despite his deafness, Daddy talked as best he could. We all learned the ABC's of sign language so we could converse in our own family way.

"I have a right fine card here," I told her, holding it up. "Can I wear my Easter Rabbit hat? The pink hat with the rabbit ears we made yesterday. Momma, can I wear it, pleee-ase?"

"First, put it on and let me see how you look because we don't want to scare any of those old folks at the Happy Acres half to death. Aunt Annabelle has only been living there since last fall. We don't want them to kick her out of what is going to be her last home on our account."

I grabbed only the most wonderful Easter hat I had ever seen in my entire life. Although it was made of pink construction paper, I knew it would probably sell for at least a dollar or two in Meridian.

Any rabbit would be proud to wear this hat.

"Ready to go?" Momma asked.

I continued to straighten my rabbit ears to make sure the black whiskers and cotton-ball nose were lined up with my very own.

"Jus-ta about," I called back to her, running into the hall with my rabbit ears flopping. "Momma, does our Great Aunt Annabelle ever get lonely living without family around her? Did she miss seeing us Easter Sunday or not?"

"Remember now, she's got other old folks around her to keep her company. Yesterday, I wanted to go visit her, but sometimes I hate to put us through more loneliness. Besides, your daddy was sobering up from Saturday night. At home at least, if he shows out like he does when he's liquored up with moonshine whiskey, we can handle him."

I listened, knowing what she meant. I knew it was us three. We were alone in Meridian save for whatever we filled our days and nights with which was music and storytelling.

Laughing, she bounced one of my pink ears a little. "Babydoll, you look as cute as a ladybug! I don't care if your rabbit hat does scare a couple of those old folks, you can wear it anyway." She bent down and kissed my cheek and shook her car keys signaling me to hurry up.

"Thank you, Momma."

"I'm glad you are not sick and coughing with the bronchitis. Breech babies are so delicate. Always sick. I pray every chance I get to the good Lord that you will grow stronger. Go on. Choose a greeting card so we can go."

The greeting card I chose had a field with thousands of tiny yellow wildflowers that lay like carpet across it from east to west. And right in the middle was a shack that looked like someone had forgotten about it because it looked as deserted as an empty ant bed. The weeping willow trees that surrounded the shack were caught up in a breeze while some of their long flowing branches held onto the shack like guardian angels.

If those weeping willow trees could talk, I bet they would tell Great Aunt Annabelle what memories that shack held for them.

I grabbed a colored ink pen, reached out onto my screenless, open bedroom windowsill for my cat, Kitty Momma. The best thing about Kitty Momma was she always gave the appearance that she knew *exactly* what was going on by the way she cut her golden oval eyes around at folks when they were talking. It was like she had a special *want* in her eyes, as if she was filled with hunger for more than food. No matter if folks were talking about the weather, President John F. Kennedy, Jesus Christ, the price of cotton, or how much butter was in a pound cake, Kitty Momma acted as if she understood them.

"Myra Boone, you put that cat back outside right now! Come on. Let's go before it gets any hotter."

Getting up from my chair with her under my right armpit steady as a freight train of cotton on its way to Atlanta, I said, "Kitty Momma, we'll be back after a while." I kicked open the front screen door and let her free.

While looking towards a mimosa tree, I thought of how Daddy would tease me with slurred, broken speech while I sat on his lap in the cool of the day as the Mississippi sky would turn from blue to pink to purple then to black. I would lean on his chest and eat raisins. The ones that came in the red box with the sunshine over the Indian's head. Momma was always close by our side rocking in her chair and humming a country song or a gospel tune while he told us stories about his life back in Saint Augustine, Florida. Daddy would tell of his best friend, Ray Charles Robinson, and their times together in the summer solstices of mid-June. Ray was his only connection to the world outside of Meridian. He was "Brother Ray" to Daddy.

"Babydoll, stop with your daydreaming! Come on now. Let's hit the road and write." Momma grabbed her purse and took me by the hand, and we flew out the front door like two ribbons blowing in the wind.

IT WAS A LAZY MONDAY MORNING. The Mississippi air was packed full of stale heat popping with humidity. I saw a redbird singing on the limb as we drove past another mimosa tree a few minutes from our house. Since I had been told redbirds were made for wishing, I made a wish that everybody at Happy Acres would like my Easter rabbit hat.

"Myra, look over toward the Philadelphia courthouse," Momma said. Philadelphia was known far and wide as the Neshoba County seat and was forty miles from Meridian.

Rolling down my window and sticking my hand halfway out for the wind to glide off the top of my bent fingers and maybe cool down my face a little, I asked, "Why?"

"I want you to see the trees in the brightness of the early morning sun."

I let my eyes absorb the sight of the courthouse as the sun painted the giant oaks in colors of maroon and gold amid the white and lilac glory of the crepe myrtles. The sight of the old courthouse in the early morning light made me feel like it was a frozen moment in time during the Civil War era I'd heard told about.

"Babydoll, did you know when Mister William Faulkner visited Philadelphia, he swore on the Holy Bible the monument of the Confederate soldier on the grass, right over there, came to life and walked with him through the courtyard and they shared Civil War stories and a bottle of scotch whiskey?"

"Really?" I asked, wondering who in the world she was talking about.

"That's the story he told."

I shrugged then smiled.

"Babydoll, what *inspires* you?"

"*Inspires me?*" I asked as my rabbit ears blew in the wind.

"What *stirs* your heart?"

"I see nature and animals surrounded by springtime," I said.

"What lifts up your spiritman?"

"My *spiritman?*"

"Myra, we all have an inner voice that lifts us up or brings us down. The still small voice that speaks to our heart. The voice you can feel and sometimes hear," she informed me.

"Like when my conscience tells me the difference between right and wrong?"

"Exactly! You must trust it and not be afraid to listen. Let it guide you."

I frowned.

Smiling, she said, "Use your *imagination* to find *inspiration*."

I felt like I was being caught up in a cloud. I closed my eyes and allowed myself to feel the smoothness of the tires now lulling us along Mississippi Highway 45 also known as the Lost Highway. When I opened them again, I began to scribble a poem verse inside the greeting card. Momma drove on, glancing from the road to me, smiling all the while.

"I want to be a bonafide writer," I declared. "Can I learn writing in school?"

And like always, when the word *school* was mentioned, Momma ignored my question. I knew as long as she lived, I'd never get to go. School was forbidden. She said the Lord didn't want me to be exposed to worldly sins taught from books found inside a schoolhouse and published outside the United States of America. I was so behind in formal book-learning I was afraid I'd never get caught up. Still, I believed the Lord for a miracle that I'd get to go learn like the rest of the children in Meridian. I wanted to make friends too. My only friends were animals and old people.

"Seems to me you already are one," she told me in an encouraging voice that made me sparkle inside with the feelings was a *somebody*. Even though I'd been told God made the rich and the poor, I knew too I was an only and lonely poor child stuck in Mississippi always worrying about everything every second of every minute of every hour of every day that nobody gave a hell about save for my folks. That's what I believed anyway.

Momma reached and turned on the car radio, and Ray Charles was singing our favorite song. As we rode on, we sang *You Are My Sunshine* along with Ray. We would always look at each other before singing: "'*Please, dear God, don't take my sunshine*, You, away'" and laugh then smile.

Even though she wouldn't let me go to school, I knew I had the best momma in the world.

Music: blues, gospel, rockabilly, country, jazz, and even rock-n'-roll on the radio saved us from being lonely. It not only lifted our spirits but was one of the few things that made us feel good about ourselves. Besides, singing was something we could do together. Momma told me if music couldn't cheer a body up, then he must be dead. Music made us smile. Music made us happy.

Momma looked over at me, took one hand off the steering wheel, pointed to my head and smiled. I reached to feel to see if the cotton nose was still on my rabbit hat. I thought of how wonderful it would be if Daddy could hear us sing or even me read what I'd written. I caught a hazy glimpse of him in my mind wearing his carpenter overalls ordered from the Sears, Roebuck and Company catalog along with a carpenter's hat that he wore to cover up his ears like he could hide his deafness. Even though Daddy was born with very little hearing, when it came to music, he could feel its beat and make out some of the songs he'd somehow memorized. To me, he looked smart as the rest of us riding down the road in his rainbow-painted pickup truck singing to himself in his own silent world, drunk or sober.

It was me who named his truck The Rainbow. He thought I was the funniest thing ever. He said it was the perfect name because when it was filled with moonshine whiskey, the sales added money towards him filling a pot of gold. I knew Daddy did the best he knew how to make two nickels so he could click them together for us. Yet, even at eleven, I sensed he was a lonely man. In Meridian, we were all lonely even in The Rainbow. We were living in a hopeless place.

Wiping the sweat from her forehead with a hanky covered in daisies, Momma broke into my thoughts, "Myra, on the day you were born, I made a deal with God."

Sitting up straighter to listen, "A *deal*?"

"Yes. I almost lost you at birth. If it hadn't had been for my neighbors, I would have died too. Your daddy wasn't home to take me to the Methodist Hospital."

"Where was he?"

"Out drinking. After all, it was Christmas Eve."

"Oh."

"Like I've told you before, you could have died from being a breech baby. I knew how much your daddy wanted a baby. He said a man has to have a child to be known as a man. I knew some way, somehow, I had to get you here to make him happy. I promised the good Lord if He would let you be born alive, I would turn you directly over to Him."

"What's a *breech* baby?"

"You were turned the wrong way and coming out of my body with your feet instead of your head first."

"Oh," I said, trying to picture my own birth. "What in the world would the Lord want with me?"

"I don't know, but the deal was made. Furthermore, I asked the Lord to let you be born normal so you could have a hand in your daddy's healing from deafness and love for the whiskey bottle and to pray the prayer of faith for him to change. I thought maybe then we could live in Goodlife," she told me with earnest.

For years, I'd been my momma's best friend. Even though I was a child, she'd told me all her secrets. I knew all too good and well she missed the love she and her family had once shared in Goodlife. Even though I'd never had any relatives around me, sometimes I missed what I didn't have, and other times I was content living in my imagination, hoping to turn our lonely yesterdays into happy todays so we could have a good life. I dreamed about that a lot.

"Momma, what can I do for the Lord to heal Daddy's ears and help him stop drinking whiskey? Tell me right now and I'll do it!"

"The Bible says all it takes is the faith of a child for a prayer to be answered. You are a child, so all you have to do is believe with enough faith. Then ask the Lord to heal him of his deafness and drinking so the Boone family can throw away its sadness."

"What about his weekend drinking and running moonshine too? That makes us sad too."

"Every man I've ever known, save for my own Poppa, ran either moonshine, whiskey or both. That's a demon Virgil Boone cannot deal with on his own. I learned years ago not to ask any man to make a promise he can't keep. When we were first married, I begged him to quit drinking. He promised he would quit it time and time again, but all promises were broken. That's one reason Momma and Poppa didn't want me to marry him. They knew what kind of life I would have with a man who drinks. Said he was worthless and in time, I'd be worthless too. Babydoll, very few men can lay down the whiskey bottle, let alone give up their tobacco, on their own, that is," she told me in earnest.

"Then, tell me. When do I pray the prayer of faith for Daddy to hear and quit drinking?" I tried to picture Daddy hearing and not wearing his carpenter's hat and us living in the city of Goodlife with Momma's own people around us.

"I don't know, but when the time is right to set your mind and believe the Lord for a miracle healing, you, and only you, will know," she said, winking like we had a secret.

"I can believe! I'll do anything so Daddy can hear me tell him I love him," I said, feeling like I had been given a blank piece of paper that was aching for words.

Momma smiled as big as the Mississippi River.

"Then, can we move to Goodlife where no one will ever be sad and lonely again? Can I go to school too?" I asked.

No answer came though save for the faint sound of Momma punching the gas pedal that moved the Ford, our greeting card that held my first poem verse, and us on towards Happy Acres.

THE FAIR

Chapter 3

MOMMA AND I had been singing with the radio and pressing through the Mississippi heat on Lost Highway 45 when I looked out the car window and saw the Neshoba County fairground buildings. They were empty until late July, when they would shed their dust covers and un-board their windows as Philadelphia to the North and Meridian to the South would explode with the much-awaited Neshoba County Fair. This cycle of progress had been coming around for a hundred or more years.

At the county fair are painted ponies, goats, tiger, deer, lions, and lambs helping to create an endless circle of joy for everyone. But nothing outshines the Dentzel Carousel with its twenty-eight animals. Two are abreast and two are chariots. The twenty-eight animals include a lion, a tiger, two deer, two antelopes, two giraffes, and twenty horses fill its thirty-foot-long revolving house. All hand-carved of brass and poplar wood. A top its crown are colorful oil paintings. It stays in operation Tuesday through Saturday all year long. Our carousel is one of the best because it has all its original animals. A ride costs five cents.

Through open windows across the dusty clay grounds, fair music drifted from the carousel house as the air mingled the smells of popcorn, cotton candy, and laughter. Any passerby could catch a glimpse of the heart and soul of Philadelphia with the sense of vigor and progress that only a fair can bring to a small town. Every summer since I was four, we went to see the high school bands with red, white, and blue ribbons draped all over their hats like tiny American flags. And the Ferris wheel could be seen, no matter where anyone stood, with its rainbow of colors continuously blinking to create a perfect circle of lights.

“Momma, can we drive through the fairgrounds?” I asked.

Slowing down, she said, “Why in the world would you want to drive through a ghost town of all things?”

"I would like to ride the carousel and see how it feels without the visitors there. I want to see if I am *inspired*."

Smiling, Momma said, "Babydoll, what have you done with the greeting card?"

"It's right here," I told her, admiring the words I had so patiently printed inside its flap in colored ink.

"Well, don't lose it. Hear? Since the fairgrounds are behind Happy Acres, I suppose we can make a little detour so you can ride the carousel. You got a nickel handy?"

Our Ford breezed on through the front gate of the fairground.

Smiling, "Why, no. You'll have to loan me one."

"I reckon I can spare a nickel. Oh, no, Myra, today is Monday. The carousel is only open Tuesday through Saturday. We are *one day* too late."

But we couldn't turn back from the fair's entrance gate. Then as quick as a rain cloud bursts without warning, a man in a wheelchair appeared on the other side of the gate. I looked over to Momma as fast as she glanced over my way, but neither of us said a word when he proclaimed from his wheelchair, "Halt! The fair is not open today."

"What in the name of God is he doing?" Momma asked me.

He was dressed in his Sunday best, no doubt about it, and holding onto a Bible as if his life depended on it. The hard, bitter look on his old worn-out face scared me to death until I noticed his beautiful arctic blue eyes that moved like ocean waves.

"It's family!" yelled our Great Aunt Annabelle.

"*Great day in the morning!*" Momma proclaimed about to faint.

"It's my niece, Marigold, and her girl, Myra Boone. The good Lord done gone and had mercy on me and sent some of my own kin to help us! Saint Peter Simpson, you let them pass on through the gate." Great Aunt Annabelle continued giving out orders while Saint Peter waved us on through the gate with a Bible.

"How in the world did you all get out here?" Momma asked when a half a dozen other old-timers began to move through the fresh, red orange Mississippi clay and approach the Ford.

"We walked!" my Great Aunt Annabelle replied.

"Well, I know you walked! What is that Colored man doing down on his knees?"

I butted in, "I think he is praying. Is this the new fair called Progress?"

The Colored man was on bended knees, praying in the carousel house right beside a lion, "Hear me, Sweet Jesus. Hear me when I cry with my voice. Hide not thy face from me and don't put thy servant,

Wilbur Legshoe, away in anger like all the others done gone and did when they put me out at Happy Acres with just me clothes on me back! Sweet Jesus, You have truly been me help. So far, so good. Jud'st grants me the grace to get through another blue Mississippi Monday. Sweet Jesus, please jud'st help me git the hell out of Happy Acres before I have to set it a-fire!"

"Look-y here, brothers and sisters," Great Aunt Annabelle proclaimed. "They have come to break bread with us after all, but they are *one day* too late."

"But they did come," said a voice.

"Did you bring us any fruit?" Great Aunt Annabelle asked.

"I would like to have an ice-cold Coke-a-Cola!" another voice cried out.

"*Daughter of Eve*," whispered a wicked voice.

"I want me some vanilla cream," the Colored man cried out.

"Aunt Annabelle, I asked you a question!" Momma yelled, scaring me.

"Who's Eve?" I asked the sky.

No answer.

Looking down at me fumbling with my rabbit ears, an old Colored lady who didn't have a tooth in her head asked, "Child, you are *one of us*, ain't you?"

"I suppose so," I answered her, not sure if I was supposed to or not.

"My Lord in heaven," Momma said, shaking her head. "Don't scare my child half to death!"

"They aren't. I'm fine," I told her, scared we'd have to leave if I acted afraid.

"We ain't gonna hurt nary a soul! Are we?" cried a voice.

"You got that right!" an old lady hollered out from back behind a booth with *Cotton Candy and Candied Apples 10 cents-a-piece* painted in black across its front. With a wicked smile, she asked soft and low, "Honey Bunny, how about some sweet stuff after your Easter

dinner?"

"Don't pay her a dime!" Great Aunt Annabelle cried out as some other old lady joined in and said, "That's wise advice because I bought her last sack of cotton candy, and Saint Peter Simpson over at the gate is a-peeling his candied apple even as we speak."

"Why in the world is he peeling a candied apple?" I asked.

"He has a set of them old wooden teeth from way back and can't chew well," the old lady confessed. He waved to us with his butcher knife. It had a blood red handle made of wood.

"I think I am going to faint," Momma said.

Another stranger came up and began to fan her with an old, stained envelope. The stranger winked over at me and smiled.

"Where did he get that butcher knife?" Momma asked. After no answer came, she turned as pale as a ghost.

"I used to play the piano," someone told his neighbor.

Momma was looking better and had some color back in her face when, "*Blast! Pop! Pop!*" rang out from another booth as the entire crowd of old-timers began to scatter, marking the fresh red orange Mississippi clay with hundreds of confused footprints.

"Jesus Christ!" cried a voice.

"Where?" asked another voice.

"*Great day in the morning!*" the Colored man proclaimed, still inside the carousel. He was sitting on the lion.

Listen, I heard a voice whisper.

Then, as if it were a long ago, everyone looked young again like me. Seemingly, I was outside myself looking at the shells of their earthly bodies. I saw the souls of everyone at the fair. Not a single soul held a hue of color. Everyone was the same.

"How in the world did Buddy Boy get a gun is what I would like to know?" Great Aunt Annabelle asked, breaking into my thoughts.

"Maybe it was left over from a war," I answered.

"What war?" she asked me.

"The Civil War!" shouted Wilbur Legshoe.

"Oh, dear God in heaven!" Momma cried out.

"Where's me Master?" the Colored man asked and jumped from the lion's back, ran from the carousel, and looked all around the fairground.

My mind and imagination took me back in time to a Louisiana bijou where the Colored man was young again standing beside a beautiful white pregnant girl. She was standing behind a white, regal antebellum mansion that bore the name *Valley of the Shadows* where marching would-be soldiers were intent upon overtaking it. I saw a mimosa tree blowing amid an evening breeze. I smelled its pink flowers before the breeze turned black with screams filled with pain and blood. When more of the sweet smell of mimosa came back to me, the Colored man asked, "Where's the baby? Did me Master drown me first-born son in a cotton sack like he did all the other baby boys?"

I saw the beautiful white girl sobbing and rubbing her bare red breast. I felt my head spin when I saw a group of pearly-white men dressed in long white sheets led by a man swinging a blazing stick of wood while waving a cotton sack. I heard a baby screaming like it was sick or hungry or lost.

"They told me it wuz a dead kitten, but I know'd the truth... Why didn't somebody save me baby boy? Moses!"

"I found the gun in an empty booth," Buddy Boy announced, and brought me back to the fair. He slithered across the soggy red orange clay, reached up, and then he picked an apple from a nearby tree.

Saint Peter Simpson screamed like a rabbit before skinning, "Aaaaaaaa! Aaaaaaaa! Don't shoot me! Don't shoot me!"

The Colored man ran like a streak of lightning over to comfort Saint Peter Simpson.

"Sweet Jesus! What's the matter with him?" Momma asked the old folks.

"Saint Peter Simpson was shot by his first and only wife after she caught him in the *act* without her! And to hear him tell it, he thought he was a perfect man up until that point in his life. He sure enough hates guns or any kind of popping noises. We all know that by now. Did you all know we are in one of them old folks' homes? Well, we is in Happy Acres!" the first old lady proclaimed.

"Lord, send the fire!" Buddy Boy cried out, taking a bite from his apple.

"Don't you all fret nary a bit because I will calm Saint Peter's nerves with this here Holy Bible," the Colored man stated, taking the Bible from Saint Peter Simpson's lap but not before Saint Peter Simpson read, "The Lord is my Shepherd; I shall not want."

"Yes, the Lord says in His Word that He knows what we need before we even ask it. So, go on and read to Saint Peter. Ask him what he needs from heaven," our great aunt encouraged him.

"Are you going to hit him over the head with it like they do at the church house?" Buddy Boy asked.

Great Aunt Annabelle shook an angry right fist at him.

"Saint Peter Simpson wants to be baptized in the River called Jordan a'fore he dies," one of them commented.

"There ain't enough water in the United States of America to baptize that evil, wicked heathen man, so he's got to go overseas to get dipped in a river there," an old lady whispered to me.

"I would love to learn how to rock ´n´ roll like that Tupelo boy," another old lady proclaimed with energy.

"You and me both, Sister! Oh, I *love* Elvis!" shouted my Great Aunt Annabelle.

Once again, Momma looked as pale as a cup of fresh cream.

"The truth jumps quick to the heart," someone stated.

"Will somebody tell me why you all are here?" Momma cried out.

Then as slow as the hands on a clock seem to move when you are a child, Great Aunt Annabelle began saying, "Marigold, let me tell why we are all at the fair."

"Tell me," Momma replied, and an old Colored woman began to fan her with an old, stained envelope once again.

"Easter was yes-ter-day. And none of us had a visitor or a place to go for Sunday dinner. Why, we all used to have old home places of our very own, but not a one of us can remember what happened to them let alone why we are all bunched up in a building with twenty-five or so beds in it as well as indoor plumbing to boot! Pain was all around us. We all got our nickels ready and hit the road with high hopes of riding the merry-go-round. You know, the carousel? But we can't find anyone to start it up for us. All we wanted to do was have a little fun. We wanted to feel loved by someone, something, anything just one more time. That's all. We wanted to feel love," she said with sadness.

"All I ask is to be left alone," someone stated.

"We thought we might find Gustav Dentzel because he was the Pennsylvanian who spent seven years building the carousel way back between 1892 and 1899. But he ain't here either," Buddy Boy said, while the others continued to look and wander aimlessly about the fairgrounds.

"Child, I never asked to be left alone," the Colored lady whispered to me. When I looked into her face, I saw a young girl much like myself only with black skin.

"How did you get past the alarm?" Momma asked her.

"Saint Peter Simpson told us how to break it," she answered with a smile.

"Saint Peter Simpson's really good at gett'n loose and all. He told us about all them times he got away from his old lady before she shot him 'tween the legs and put his light out!" the first old lady chuckled, giving Saint Peter Simpson a wave of appreciation over towards the entrance gate. He waved back to us with an apple in one hand and a butcher knife in the other.

"Saint Peter says he used to have s-e-x on the brain until he got a revelation," one of them commented.

"Good God Almighty! Don't you talk like *that* in the front of my child!" Momma yelled.

"And we walked out the door," Great Aunt Annabelle informed us.

All the other members of her group began to assemble themselves around us once again.

"Little girl, would you like an apple now?" Buddy Boy asked me, smiling.

I shook my head no.

"Anyway, here we all are," Great aunt Annabelle began, and then introduced her friends. "This is Miss Emily, Pearly, Gladys, Bertha, Buddy Boy, Wilbur Legshoe, and you know who Saint Peter Simpson is by now anyway," she added, nodding over to him.

Still, he was parked in his wheelchair guarding the front gate holding a Bible in one hand and a butcher knife in the other. His face looked hard and distant save for his cold but moving arctic blue eyes.

"Did you finish your apple?" Miss Pearly called out to him.

"Hell, yeah! I used to be a ladies' man until," Saint Peter began.

Gladys spoke up, "Until he found a friend in Jesus! Annabelle, what about us mailing this here Rossville letter?"

"I plumb forgot about the letter!" Great Aunt Annabelle shouted then added, "It's all I have left in the way of a family. It's a letter from my Rossville kin. I wanted to mail it to my dear Andrew because I knew I wouldn't be seeing him, Easter. I wanted to share it with him. It's all I got left in this whole wide world besides this old worn out body."

"Is he dead?" the Colored man, Wilbur Legshoe, asked her

respectful-like while removing his hat before placing it over his heart.

"Lord in heaven, no!" she proclaimed.

"Why didn't he come to visit yes-ter-day?" Gladys asked.

"Because he is with the Lord," she replied.

"Well, that's the only other good reason I know of for not getting out on Easter Sunday," Wilbur Legshoe informed us while replacing his hat.

"How in the world do you expect him to get this letter then?" Miss Gladys asked with true concern.

There was no answer from anyone as Momma hung her head and the tears began to flow down her cheeks like the river of life.

I remembered our greeting card and said, "Well, we brought you a right fine card here."

"Didn't you all have visitors yesterday, either?"

No answer.

"Sweet Marigold, for goodness's sake now, don't you cry another tear because we all have got each other! The merry-go-round will start back up any minute, won't it?" Great Aunt Annabelle said in a faster voice than she had begun with while holding up a Buffalo nickel.

"Great Aunt Annabelle, I have written a poem verse for you," I told her, feeling ashamed of myself but not quite sure as to why.

"Let's have a look at it," Miss Pearly said, looking around at the other old folks who were gathering closer to us by the second.

"I have it right here," I said, reaching into the pocket of my dress for the yellow greeting card.

"You got any black and whites to show us?" a voice asked.

"No, not today," Momma answered, wiping her eyes with her daisy hanky.

"Woo-hoo! I bet you got a camer-y withe you!" one of them said.

"Miss Myra, I want me one of them Easter rabbit hats like yours," Miss Emily told me.

I smiled and handed Great Aunt Annabelle the greeting card.

Everyone gathered around us except for Saint Peter Simpson who was still guarding the front entrance gate like a Roman soldier.

"My Lord in heaven!" shouted Miss Emily while all the others drew in closer to see. "It's my old home place right on the front of the card, it surely is," she said in earnest.

"Ain't either! It's mine!" shouted the Colored one.

"It's my home place! It's my home place!" Miss Pearly commenced to shout while the others moved closer to the greeting card.

Great Aunt Annabelle said, "It is not nary one of our home places because the hallmark right here on the back of the card says, "Shack on the Old Natchez Parkway near the Trace thought to be where the post riders rode on the Pony Express route in 1860."

"The Natchez Trace was a tunnel that ran through the forests and made for early American travelers," Wilbur Legshoe stated.

Miss Emily smiled over to Wilbur Legshoe.

"Shoot, I bet that very shack was where some of them *Pony Express* riders stopped on their way to Nashville, Tennessee, to rest!" Miss Emily rang out, and the others nodded.

"Marigold Davis Boone," Great Aunt Annabelle said. Everyone gathered around us so close you couldn't have squeezed a flea in if you had tried. "This is about the nicest greeting card that I have ever seen in all my born days. It's yellow like the sunshine!"

"Well, you all need to thank Myra because she's the one who picked it out and wrote the poem verse while I was explaining to her about inspiration. She's been reading and writing since she was about four. I spend a lot of time teaching her myself," Momma told them.

I smiled then said, "Momma taught me how to write when I was four. She was a Sunday School teacher over in Soso."

"Why, I declare," my great aunt said, shaking her head.

"Open it and read what Myra wrote," Momma suggested.

My great aunt opened the card and read aloud to her friends from the inside flap the capital letters I had so patiently printed and misspelled while I crossed my fingers under my left arm for luck that she would read my poem verse aloud.

She read:

Nature's Conversation

"Good news, Green Spring, Green Spring!" shouted a
Hummingbird as it flew in on the Wind.
"Why, it's the best news I've ever heard," buzzed a Bee.
"Are you two talking to me?" asked a Tree.
"Green Spring, Green Spring! What a glorious ring. Such a
beautiful thing," sang a Bird.
"What a delight," said the Day to the Night Who added
sadly, "Winter has blown away."
The Sun beamed down to the Earth. "Your little ones are filled
with such pleasure. That nothing could measure!"
In rushed the Sea with, "Hey, everyone, wait for me!"

"Let all God's creations sing: "Green Spring, Green Spring!

For Fall will soon be on its way."

An Ant whispered, "I see God's magnificence all around."

"Now ain't she a smart child? Are you sure you don't want an apple?" Buddy Boy asked with a soothing voice while slithering up the apple tree again to pick a fresh piece of fruit for me.

"I'm sure," I said, standing my ground.

"She's an *only* child," Momma told them.

"I'm eleven going on twelve." I stated, then added, "My birthday is December 25."

"And it is written in red ink," Wilbur Legshoe marveled.

"Let me be the first to wish you a very merry happy birthday!" Miss Gladys shouted.

I laughed.

"I'm a hundred years older than you," one lady told me.

Saint Peter Simpson squealed out once again like a lamb on its way to the slaughter.

Miss Emily stated, "He feels left out of our conversation. And besides, we had better get him on back to his room because he nor did nary-a-one of us take our medicine this morning when the fat nurse came around to give it."

"Shut your trap! Don't go and tell off on the rest of us!" my Great Aunt Annabelle cried out, shaking a threatening finger at Miss Emily.

"Well, it's the truth," the Colored man said, taking up for Miss Emily.

"Thank you kindly, Brother Wilbur Legshoe," she told him, cutting Great Aunt Annabelle a look like you would expect to see on a face when you entered a ghost town.

"And how in the world did you all get out of taking your medicine?" Momma rang out with alarm.

"Let me tell it! Let me tell it!" Gladys shouted before saying, "At about 6:30 this morning when the nurse with the big behind came around with all our pills, we held 'em under our tongues. That is, we all did 'cept for Saint Peter 'cause like we told you before, he has had a set of old wooden teeth, so he held his pills between his teeth. Then, we all threw them into the indoor contraption called a *commode*. Ain't that right?" she said to the others.

"For the most part," Miss Pearly agreed.

"Except for one thing," Wilbur Legshoe said. "They is devil pills that take away our minds!"

"Amen!" they all cried in unison while some of them waved their arms in the air towards the eastern sky.

"What in the world can we do now?" Momma asked them, starting to tear up. "It's my fault. We should have come to see you on Easter."

"Can you read or spell?" I asked my great aunt.

"I read your poem verse aloud, didn't I? My spelling has always been right good," she replied, pleating her bottom lip.

"Momma, let's take her on back home to Meridian with us. We have an extra bedroom. Besides, I need the *inspiration* she can offer me. You know I need a reading and spelling teacher to help along with my writing when you are cooking," I suggested amid my feelings of shame and confusion that I'd never been to school.

With my words, my great aunt's face lit up like the sun. And when our eyes met, I saw the same *want* that Kitty Momma had in her eyes when she was half-starved for something more than food.

"Babydoll, why that's the best idea you have ever had! But we'll have to ask your daddy first," Momma told me.

Great Aunt Annabelle asked, "Marigold, can your Virgil hear yet?"

Momma answered with, "Virgil can faintly hear sometimes. He sings and dances every chance he gets. He still sits outside for hours while the truck radio blares. He tries his best to listen and sing with me on the box radio. He still drinks more so on the weekends nowadays. Nothing my Virgil does makes good sense. That doesn't change my love for him though."

Great Aunt Annabelle said with enthusiasm, "That won't bother me nary a bit because I don't make good sense half the time myself! Hey, I love to talk and dance and sing! And I can cook too. The Lord is able to heal us of our sicknesses and weaknesses if we be willing."

"Momma, can you *feature* all that?" I asked with excitement.

"She sho' enough can do it all," Wilbur Legshoe said, while all her friends shook their heads in total agreement and looked right happy-like at her.

"What's that roaring sound I hear?" Miss Pearly asked, bending an ear toward the sky.

"Do you reckon it's your Andrew coming for you or his letter?" Buddy Boy asked, back on the ground again.

Gladys reached over and handed my great aunt the old, stained envelope.

"I don't know what that noise is," Great Aunt Annabelle replied. The envelope fell from her hands onto the red orange clay beneath our feet.

I reached down and picked it up.

"Maybe it's the Lord!" a voice announced.

Whispers filled the air.

Then, I heard a noise like a great rush of wind approaching us. The old folks all turned around at the same time to see what they too had heard. A familiar colorful truck bounced a little in the air on past Saint Peter Simpson in his wheelchair. It picked up speed and went on by us like a sparrow on the wings of the north wind flying straight into springtime.

"Marigold, ain't that your Virgil riding on a rainbow?" our great aunt asked us.

Please, dear Lord God, let me see my daddy's smiling face so that I can ask him to take us on home.

I closed my eyes and prayed feeling something like a fire starting deep down inside my heart as I took hold of my Great Aunt Annabelle's old worn-out hand with all the hope and strength an eleven-year-old girl can muster up to let her know she had somebody left in this old world to love her again. Together, we held tight to her old, stained envelope and new yellow greeting card.

When I opened my eyes, I saw it was my daddy riding in The Rainbow singing to himself while swinging his head from side-to-side, never once to take his eyes off Lost Highway 45. He didn't even catch a glimpse of us. My Easter rabbit hat blew off and went on turning in the wind like the Ferris wheel and blowing straight towards the center of the fairgrounds. It flew into the empty pink, lavender, blue, yellow, and red buildings that had been standing for a hundred or more years.

THE LETTER

Chapter 4

THE MONDAY AFTER the Easter Sunday we helped our Great Aunt Annabelle Davis Stringer escape from the Happy Acres Nursing Home, I taught her the ABC's of sign language so not nary a soul would feel left out of any of our family conversations. Truth be told, I was happy to have another voice around me. For hours, Kitty Momma and I'd listen to her tell stories about her yesteryears. The only thing we had in common was that neither of us had ever been to school. We copied words from books while pretending we understood them. She could read some though. The first thing she read to me was an old family letter from Rossville, Tennessee.

October 7th 1887

Piney Woods, Rossville, Tennessee 38066

Attention: Eloy + Martha Shows Stringer

Goodlife, Mississippi 39437

Dear Eloy and Martha

I today write to answer yours of August 20th which I was very sorry to hear you had been sick but was glad to hear you was gettin' well. There have been some bad sickness here but none of our connection is sick. Some deaths here. Elisha's little girl Sarah died by a few days ago. Poly's brother Sam's baby Mary died.

Your Aunt Poly has another boy which make seven boys. They names are Elisha, Sherman, Cornelius, Joseph, Henry, Von, and little Joseph Lester, the baby. We have one girl, Virginia. So you see, we have a large family of eight and like most of the po' folks blessed with children. It be a great responsibility to raise them right if they be willing.

We are having very dry weather here now, not much rain since the first of August. Crops of corn, good cotton, 3/4 peas, hardly any sugar cane. Sorry potatoes with 1/2 crop of good pindars made. Very sorry hogs. So you see our chance for the year is not good. With all this, I feel that we have been blessed. We have had no storm or earthquake or other bad disaster. I traveled to sell cotton last week. I got $8.80. I bought more seed at $8.25. Sheeting be at 5 *cent a yard. Little money goes a long way if we use it wisely in our town where 127 folk live.*

We have but one place where liquor is sold in this county. There is no dry men of our folks but me and Elisha. The rest fight for whiskey and some get bad drunk. Our neighbor got a-hold of a bad batch of Alabama moonshine and they found him dead up around a waterfall near the Piney Woods Creek bank with his head bent over in the water. It was a sad day as he had four children and another on the way. He was buried with his Bible.

Some folks belong to the church. Some are hard shells with only one hard shell preacher. Some Missionary Baptists and many Methodists.

Our news is that Aunt Poly is aimed to go make the trip to the Salem Camp Meeting over your way in Mississippi with her Poppa soon. Aunt Poly say they will call on you then. They will be tenting like always. Her folks been making the trip since 1860. She say two meetings were shut down only cause of the Civil War and the yellow fever. Her mind is made. I reckon the children will go along. Me and Elisha will work hard to finish in the fields. The women seem to want to go for praying and fellowship of kin. Aunt Poly say the baby little Joseph Lester do need a healing if it be the Lord's will. She say the Holy Ghost is thickest over there, making anything possible. The baby was born with a big head. He cry all the time. He ain't just right. He sad. We sad. Even our old dog Smarty is sad. Aunt Poly say only the Lord can heal him.

Most folks here is right pleased with the way that President Grover Cleveland is running the country. He do the best he can do with what be passed along to him from Chester A. Arthur and his heavy drinking bunch.

We saw the Statue of Liberty on the front page of a paper to be dedicated along a great body of water.

Fenton Laurel has been appointed to Administer on your grandma's estate. The Lord be willing then we will all get a fair shake.

I would like to get a little extra money so that I can start with some bees for honey making to sell pint jars along the roadside. That be my prayer to happiness and feeding my family of ten.

I shall register this letter. I send you ten dollars so that sets us even. Write soon as you get this. Your Aunt Poly say write how many children you all have and their names. Also tell Lorena, Annabelle, Reatha, and Martha to write the news. We glad to hear from you any time. So nothing more save for I remain your loving brother,

John Davis Shows in Rossville, Tennessee.

"KITTY MOMMA, can you *feature* all that?" I said with amazement to my white cat I'd raised since birth.

Great Aunt Annabelle smiled. Reading the letter to me always made her happy.

"What's a *pindar*?" I asked her.

"A peanut, I think. John Davis grew peanuts," she told me.

"Did the crying baby with the big head get its healing at the Salem Camp Meeting?"

"I don't rightly know," Great Aunt Annabelle replied, her bottom lip a pleat. She stopped speaking and looked straight at me. "Why?"

"Come October, I'd like to go to the Salem Camp Meeting so I can pray and believe the Lord for Daddy to get healed of his deafness, so we can have a good life," I told her, remembering the deal Momma made with the Lord at my birth.

Momma said I was a breech baby. She promised the Lord if He'd let me be born alive, she'd turn me over to Him. Momma told me she believed I was an answer to her prayer to have a good life. Said she knew I was to be the one to pray and believe for Daddy to be healed of his deafness. That was the mantle I was to carry on my shoulders.

"Come October," great Aunt Annabelle mused.

I smiled as Kitty Momma skittered around the room before she jumped up onto the windowsill after a red ladybug that was doing its best to squeeze its fragile legs through a tiny crack in the windowpane. The escape was completed into the early morning light which was making its way into the room one ray at a time.

It was after everyone was asleep that same night when I wrote a letter and my first poem verse while looking at a picture of a seemingly happy clown in the *Reader's Digest*. I copied the address on the Rossville letter and addressed it to the sick baby with the big head, Joseph Lester Stringer, and the old sad dog, Smarty.

I'd been using the gas heater in the living room as a play mailbox lately and out of habit, I mailed my letter and poem verse straight down its front vents. Embarrassed and beings it was between spring and summer, I decided not to tell on myself. Besides, Daddy would open it up and clean it out in the fall before the first winter's frost like he always did never to breathe a word of my misuse of it to Momma.

The Clown

The Clown makes you smile.

Even if you are not a little child.

Look!

The Clown glows.

Even her Joy shows.

See!

The Clown fills everyone with glee.

I wish the Clown was me.

—Mary Myra Boone

Mississippi-born on December 25, 1950

VOICES OF EVERY COLOR

Chapter 5

October 31, 1961

THE SALEM CAMP MEETING began with a preacher man blowing on a conch shell while yelling up towards heaven, “Let the redeemed of the Lord God say so!”

“Praise Jesus!” the crowd roared.

Will Daddy get a healing or not? I wondered, feeling the crowd’s energy.

“You got that right!” Great Aunt Annabelle hollered.

“Lord have mercy,” Momma said, looking all around the tent.

"What does *redeemed* mean?" I asked.

"Free from sin," Momma whispered, taking hold of Daddy's hand then mine.

"That ain't nary one of us!" Great Aunt Annabelle shouted, clapping her hands. "Ssssshshush," Momma said, fanning the hot night air.

"You Piney Woods pioneers let it be known where your home states be," the preacher man said, walking around the front of the tent real tall like.

"Alabama," shouted a voice.

"Georgia," came from a man in front of us.

"New Or-leeans!" shouted a woman in the back.

Everyone turned to see her.

"Tennessee," shouted my great aunt.

"Texas," said a small voice to our left.

Momma looked nervous and afraid while Daddy was taking it all in, looking trapped in a sheet of glass in his deafness while sweating like a pig. Momma had made sure he wore long sleeves to hide the color of his skin.

I wish Daddy could hear!

I looked down and noticed my new red knee socks Daddy had

bought at a boiled peanut roadside stand outside of Meridian. He teased me one leg was growing faster than the other because the sock on my left leg was about half an inch shorter than my right sock. Knowing he couldn't read; Momma and I didn't mention that they were marked *Seconds*.

The preacher man said, "We all God's children. Every color, shape, and form of man-nnn-kind be welcome in this here tent. Folks come from all-l-l-l over the South to the Salem Camp Meeting! If you find that you ain't comfortable with the way we got it set up with the 'Colored' section in the back, step on over to the 23rd cabin called the *Public Tent*."

"What's the 23rd cabin for? Are they reading the Psalms over there or what?" Great Aunt Annabelle turned and asked her neighbor from Texas.

"Nope. It's a concession stand with hotdogs and cotton candy operated by local Shriners. It was set up so in between services folks can visit, have family reunions, fill in the gaps on their genealogical charts, eat, and read the Bible at the same time. It's the rough-looking tabernacle with its own open sides and concrete floors."

"Well, how about that? Concrete, eh? I've never seen a floor made of concrete before," she said.

Suddenly, I wondered if the floors in a schoolhouse were made of concrete too.

Pointing to her left, "See it? Right over towards the center of the campgrounds. See it now? It's right over thataway?" The Texas lady continued on in reply to my great aunt's question and my unspoken observation. Then, she asked a question of her own, "Sister, you said you were from Tennessee, now, didn't you? What part?"

"Rossville, Tennessee. Of all things, food in the Lord's tent! Why, that's blasphemy! Never heard of such. Real concrete floors, eh? Why, someone in the Bible ran fools out of a temple once because they were eating and such," my great aunt recalled, shaking her head in dismay.

I wish I had some of that cotton candy.

Wanting something sweet, I looked towards the 23rd cabin hoping Daddy would notice me. He was watching people and trying to read their lips.

"I think it was Jesus who ran them out of the Temple because of gambling, not for eating and such," I told my great aunt, remembering the New Testament story.

"I don't blame him for that! My Andrew used to gamble himself back in the Great Smoky Mountains before he went to heaven. He drove me slam crazy, but I never did go as far as running him out of the house. Now I did lock him out a time or two though," she told us.

"Sister, what's your name?" the Texas lady asked.

"Annabelle. What might yours be?"

"Eudora," the Texas lady replied. After giving me a curious look, she said, "My, what a peculiar little girl. You are different, aren't you?"

"I suppose so," I said and pulled up my red knee socks while figuring I probably wouldn't get any of that cotton candy over at the 23rd tent. The choir began to assemble in the center of a wide hallway located at the front of the tent. The floor was made of dirt and pine straw. I suppose it was because we were outdoors. People were to our right sitting around fires that smelled of pinewood. Some of the men were holding pinewood torches that gave off an amber-like glow when swung.

The choir sang: *I'm redeem'd, / I'm redeeme'd, / Thro' the blood of the Lamb that was slain; / I'm redeem'd, I'm redeem'd, / Hallelujah to God and the Lamb.*

Momma took hold of my hand. The preacher man began to walk across the stage's center. Daddy was sitting down. He looked lost and on fire with his long sleeves. Suddenly, he bent over and took a drink of whiskey from a cough syrup bottle he had hidden in his sock.

"I want the twenty-two elders coming from the stock of the old Methodist church to come on up here," the preacher man said.

Men from all over the tent began to stand and walk toward him like giants.

I looked at Daddy who smiled at me while straightening his hat then he spelled, "Y-o-u o-k?"

"Yeah," I said, turning to face him.

He gave me a hug that smelled of whiskey.

"Many of you have come from all over the great state of Mississippi to ask the Lord God for something, haven't you?" the preacher man went on.

"Yes!" the crowd roared.

Bending over and shouting into the crowd the preacher man cried out, "Well, the Lord God is able!"

"Amen!" the crowd shouted back.

"If you be willing!" Great Aunt Annabelle shouted out.

Straightening back up, "I am going to ask the twenty-two elders to pass out these bonafide Prayer Tickets for you all to fill out. I want you to write out your prayer request on them so together we can take it to the Lord God in prayer," he directed us.

"Of all things. Never seen a Prayer Ticket before," Momma said covering her mouth.

"*Bonafide*," Great Aunt Annabelle put in.

"Why, I do declare," said the lady from New Orleans and repeated, "Bonafide, eh?"

"I got a writing pencil right here," I said, dipping down deep into my purse for one.

"Well, you are going to need it!" Great Aunt Annabelle said, clapping her hands. And with her clapping gesture, Daddy jumped up, ready to fight. Once Momma told him what was going on, he sat on back down and helped himself to another drink of whiskey. He looked lonely and out of place.

The twenty-two elders began to walk and hand out slips of paper to the crowd. I looked into the Colored section for Opal and Eddy, but I wasn't able to lay eyes on them. They were our Colored friends who had come with us hidden in the truck bed of The Rainbow under a lap blanket.

"I don't want you to tell your neighbor what you are writing on your Prayer Ticket. I want it to be between you and the Lord God," he went on.

"That's fair enough," Great Aunt Annabelle stated.

What to write?

An elder handed me a bonafide Prayer Ticket.

Is this the right time to make good on Momma's deal with the Lord for Daddy's healing or not?

Elbowing Momma, I asked, "Why do we only get *one* ticket? What to write?"

Winking at me, "Write what your heart tells you to write," she replied.

I knew what she wanted me to write. After all, for six months I had stood by and watched Great Aunt Annabelle make the promise to Momma come October, she would get Daddy to drive us to the Salem Camp Meeting so I could pray for Daddy to get healed from his deafness and drinking. We agreed not to breathe a word of our intentions to Daddy. Otherwise, he would have never agreed to the trip. I knew in my heart it was plain as rain he'd give anything to be able to hear. I knew he'd never give up his drinking not even to be able to hear. Not for me or anyone else on God's green earth.

Motioning for us to stand, the preacher man told us, "First, I want you to get out your Bible and turn to the book of Jeremiah. Turn, if you will, to chapter one. Let's begin with verse four and read clear on down to verse nineteen. This is a story where the Lord God has a conversation with the boy Jeremiah about his doings with God."

Great Aunt Annabelle whispered down to me, “Whew, he is going to read half the night I bet.”

Daddy stood up to look onto my Bible.

“Jeremiah was a weeping prophet,” I whispered to Momma.

Nodding, Momma said, “He was lamented, I think.”

“What’s *lamented*?” I asked.

“Full of sorrow. Sad as the day is long,” she answered.

Like me.

“Remember, the voice of the Lord God is a-talking to the prophet Jeremiah in this passage,” the preacher man went on to tell us.

I marked the passage with my pencil by putting a star right next to verse four.

Smiling, Momma took the pencil from me and wrote in the date of October 31, 1961.

He read: “‘*Then the word of the Lord came unto me, saying / Before I formed thee in the belly I knew thee; and before thou camest forth out of the womb I sanctified thee, and I ordained thee a prophet unto nations...*’

“Then, Jeremiah told the Lord God, ‘You can’t be a-talking to me. No. Un-huh. Not me. Why I can’t even talk like a man yet for I am just-ah child.’ But tha’ Lord God didn’t buy Jeremiah’s excuse any more than he's going to buy your excuses folks ba-cause the Lord God went on and told him, 'Don't say, *I'm just-ah child,* ba-cause you are going to go into the kingdoms that I send you to, and when I tell you to speak, you will not be afraid nor scared, least I confound your right before their very eyes. Now they will fight you, but they won't win, for I am with thee, saith tha Lord.'"

"What does *confound* mean?" I turned and asked my great aunt.

"Break slam to pieces," she answered, her eyes filled with fear.

"Mercy!" I said but remembered the part about the Lord being *with* Jeremiah *even if* he broke him slam to pieces.

"The Lord God was preparing his servant for a difficult task and telling him to tuck in his shirttail and go forward and not to worry nary a bit, because he could rest assured the Lord his God was going to be right there along him. Folks, you have got to be willing to tuck in your shirttails and follow the voice of the Lord God like the prophet Jeremiah," he talked on.

Great Aunt Annabelle whispered down to me, "Jeremiah never could get it right. Nobody wanted to believe in him."

"Folks, if you will get busy and listen for the voice of the Lord God to speak to your hearts, you will be able to take back home what you came to the Salem Camp Meeting for. Now go on and fill out your bonafide Prayer Tickets so I can send the elders back around to collect them. We will pray over each and every one of them before we have the healing line."

I listened to my heart to see if I could hear it speaking as to what to write on my Prayer Ticket. I didn't hear any voices, but one word did enter my mind, *Life*. So, maybe because I wanted a better one for myself and to go to a school someday to learn how to honest-to-goodness read and write, I licked the tip of my pencil and printed *L-i-f-e* on my Prayer Ticket. I did feel a little selfish I didn't ask the Lord to heal my daddy's deafness or take away his thirst for whiskey or give him steady work so he wouldn't have to run moonshine in The Rainbow. When the elders came back around to collect our bonafide Prayer Tickets, I folded mine twice so no one would see what I had written before I dropped it into a scarlet velvet bag with wooden handles with a high hope for a good life outside of Meridian. I raised both my hands so the Lord would see I wanted to bring smiles to both my folks' faces now and forever.

Once again, the preacher man blew on the conch shell until the crowd grew quiet. He asked, "How many of you Piney Woods folks came here tonight to be touched by the Lord God? Raise your hands high."

He sure does sound serious about all this.

He put down his Bible once again and continued with the service by blowing on the conch shell for the third time.

Will the Lord reach down and touch me on the mouth with His hand like he did the boy Jeremiah?

I looked around the tent and noticed there was a group of Chickasaw and Choctaw Indians sitting directly to our right. I saw about twenty-five or thirty Indians. I had seen them walking the streets of Philadelphia on Saturdays doing their store-bought grocery shopping.

I bet they are from over towards the Nanih Waiya sacred mound.

MY THOUGHTS WANDERED back in time when my daddy had told me about the Nanih Waiya Mound before my Great Aunt Annabelle came to live with us. He said it was a mystical scared mound of earth that was anchored near the North Central Mississippi town called Noxapater in Winston County. He said the American Indians always believed it was the birthplace of the first Choctaw. Some liked to be called *The People* because everybody was a *Somebody* no matter what the white man said. Nanih Waiya was the final destination of their migration.

In my imagination, I saw Nanih Waiya appear and rise out of a dry field near the scared mound like Daddy had told to me, like an "a-p-p-a-r-i-t-i-o-n," he spelled out, or "a g-h-o-s-t." He said when he and Ray Charles were at a Florida home for boys one Friday night some of the boys had borrowed the keys to a truck and hightailed it on up to Nanih Waiya. Once there, they drove over a narrow country road to reach the great mound of earth that was right about 25 feet tall, 140 feet wide and at least 220 long. When Daddy saw it for the first time, he hollered out, "Nah-nah-nah!Wa-wa-wa ya-ya-ya! Taa-taa-taa-ha-tt nnn-nnn-nnn-oo-tt-rarara-el! Juju-stst soso-mememe-nnn-ththth-ing yyy-yyy-yyy-ou-ou-ou-rrr imimim-aaa-gin-aaa-tion fufufu-elel-eded bbb-yyy whis-whis-whis-key haha-sss con-con-jujuju-red-red uuu-uuu-uuu-pp!"

It was Ray Charles who confirmed the apparition by hollering out, "Hell yeah, Virgil, it's real! I feel it in my bones! Woo-hoo! Even though I can't see Indian smoke, I can smell it!"

Daddy told me there were two cultures of Indians that were born to two *particular* bunches who had mixed their blood together. He said it was the Chickasaw and Choctaws were the two cultures. Folks would refer to them as the twins, Mother Earth's last-born children.

My imagination took me deeper where I saw the firstborn twin,

Chickasaw, struggle up on his feet, and as soon as he was dry from being born, he began to walk away and look for a home. Daddy had said Choctaw was different from the beginning of his birth in that even though he was still wet from the journey deep within Mother Earth, he simply lay on the scared mound, drying himself in the sunshine. I knew it was true when I saw it in my imagination. I saw Choctaw naked drying in the sunshine. Once Choctaw heard Nanih Waiya, Mother Earth, crying, he waited as if he knew she would speak. Even through her tears, she pleaded to her last born, "Don't leave me."

Daddy said all Mother Earth's other children had left, leaving her afraid of growing old alone. Choctaw made a deal with his own Mother that he would never leave her if she would do one thing for him in return.

The deal: Every time Mother Earth heard the Wind's song gently moving through the leaves of the treetops, and when the Breeze began dancing through the trunks of the hardwoods and pines that were standing close guard to a stream called Joy, she would call out his name, so he could come pray to the Sky for the four seasons that made up Time: spring, summer, fall and winter. And she did. That's how Time began.

Daddy told me all the Indians needed was an imagination and a little fire water to conjure up such mystical, maddening notions. He said they had plenty of both.

THE PREACHER MAN broke into my thoughts with, "I want everyone who came here tonight for a healing from the Lord God to stand to their feet."

Folks began rising all over the tent.

Momma elbowed me in the ribs, so I stood up.

What to do now?

"Virgil, are you willing for the Lord to touch you?" Great Aunt Annabelle asked my daddy, forgetting to turn and face him, so she didn't get an answer.

"Daddy can't hear you," I spoke up.

The choir began to sing, *My God Can Do Anything.*

"Shoot, I plum forgot," she said, and didn't repeat herself.

The Bible says in the book of Isaiah that *there is no searching His understanding*. And He is *the only one* who gives power to the faint and to them that *have no might* He *increases* strength," the preacher man said.

"Amen!" roared the crowd.

"You go that right!" said a voice.

He read: "'*But they that wait upon the Lord shall renew their strength: they shall mount up wings as eagles; they shall run and not be weary; and they shall walk, and not faint.*'"

Folks clapped their hands all over the tent.

I tried to imagine myself or Momma strong as an eagle with wings of our own flying to heaven to ask the Lord for Daddy's healing but couldn't. All I could see in my mind was how happy Daddy seemed to be whether he could hear or not. I, on the other hand, was the one unhappy being so lonely and all. Even though I'd only been carrying the heavy burden of being an answer to prayer for a short while, it left me anxious from the minute I opened my eyes in the morning until I closed them again at night. I was unhappy because everyone I knew depended on me, a child, for their happiness. This left me feeling like a failure because when I was able to make them smile, it was only for a short while. Day by day, life in Meridian played on and on like a needle stuck in the worn-out grove of a vinyl record on the box radio playing itself over and over and over again. Day in and day out, every day was the same save for the change that always came with the weather. In my mind, it was as if the weather change was like the "On or Off" button on the box radio depending on the time of day. Or night. That's the best I know to describe my days and nights.

The choir sang: *My God can do it all, / My God can do it all / He will not let me fall, / He will not let me fall / No, not at all / No, not at all / My God will not let me fall.*

"How many of you have been waiting upon the Lord God?" the preacher man asked.

Again, I raised both my hands so God would see me. Looking around the Salem Camp Meeting, I saw voices of every color light up all over the tent.

"They are speaking in tongues," my great aunt whispered down to me.

How long Momma will have to wait for me to make good on my part in her deal with the Lord? I hope the Lord is looking out an open window in heaven and sees me tonight.

Suddenly, without any warning whatsoever, my Great Aunt Annabelle took hold of my hand and led me toward the front of the tent.

I turned back to look at Momma who signaled me to go forward with a nod.

Daddy said, "Gagaga-ho."

I let my great aunt direct me toward the healing line that was beginning to form. It only had a handful of people in it. My heart was beating fast and my palms were growing wet. Once again, I fixed my mind to believe the Lord would some way, somehow make the way for us to have a good life. I was ready, willing, and able to tell the preacher man too once he asked me what I wanted from the Lord.

I saw an Indian girl who was sweating and burning up with a fever right ahead of me. She was stretched out on a wooden board. Two boys with dark complexions were holding onto both sides of the board while her folks stood close by her side.

"Only the Lord God could have led you here," the preacher man said then added, "Come on and He will do the rest for you *if only* you believe."

I can believe!

I felt like I was caught up in a dream when I looked around the tent and saw a light, misty fog began to fill the night air.

I'll reach out and touch it.

Once I was brave enough to reach my hand out in front of me, I saw there was an even thicker cloud amongst us. Filled with curiosity, I reached out a second time and was able to snatch a piece of the cloud. I knew it was real when I saw something that resembled a new shoot of cotton ready for picking inside my hand. I felt like I could fly holding onto the piece of cloud.

"Myra, what in the world are you doing?" Great Aunt Annabelle asked.

"Seeing if I can hold onto the fog. I mean the cloud that's in here with us," I replied, turning to look her in the eyes.

"What cloud?" she asked, eyes searching the tent.

"Don't you see it?"

"No. I don't see it. But that doesn't mean anything. Why it must be the Holy Ghost that you see moving in the tent! Didn't my Rossville letter say it was thickest over here?" She stopped speaking, and thought a moment before saying to me, "Child, you must be a Seer."

"I see it too," the Indian girl said from her board.

"Good," I said with no questions of her.

She gave me a weak smile.

"Yes, yes, yes! They did write the Holy Ghost was the heaviest over here in my Uncle John's letter." Great Aunt Annabelle reminded me before turning loose of my other hand.

I reached down and pulled up my red knee socks, and when the Indian girl gave me yet another weak smile, the eyes of my heart saw into her life. I saw her and her folks all huddled together in one small room trying to keep warm. There was a fire roasting three squirrels on barbed wire in a makeshift fireplace off to the side of the room. They all looked older than they were. Hard even. Once the eyes of my heart released my thoughts, I tried to smile back at her, but I couldn't because she looked like she was dying.

Bending down close to her ear, I asked, "What's your name?"

"Nora," she whispered.

"I am Myra Boone," I said, reaching out to stroke her forehead.

Her forehead was so hot with fever that at once I felt a blister fester up on the tip of my pointer finger. I jerked my hand back from her forehead and shook it with hopes of cooling it while she closed both her eyes and fell asleep. When I looked at my hand, I saw the tip of my pointer finger was indeed blistered, and it scared me. I wanted to turn around and give up my place in the healing line right then and there and jackrabbit it on back to Meridian.

The choir sang while the prayer line moved forward.

My God can do it all, / My God can do it all / He will not let me fall, / He will not let me fall.

Folks began to speak in other voices unlike anything I had ever heard before while other folks began to dance all around the tent like flickering flames on an open fire. When some folks would go up to get a healing, the preacher man would reach for a bottle of sweet oil like

Momma had put in my ear when it hurt. He would take a dab of it onto his finger and reach out to touch the middle of a forehead, all the time speaking in a voice I had never heard until that night. At the moment of touch, he yelled out, "IN JESUS' NAME, I SEEK AH MIRACLE!"

We got sweet oil at the house. Why is he doing such a thing and talking in such a way?

I was amazed that folk were fainting right in front of him. Some of the twenty-two elders were standing straight behind the folks that were getting prayed for and would catch folks before they hit the ground.

I hope I don't fall out. I'm liable to break my back, then I can never go on to school because I'll be stuck in a wheelchair!

"Why are they fainting? Is the sweet oil hot?" I asked.

"Myra, they ain't fainting! That's what happens when the power of the Lord touches you. Your body can't hold it. So, you fall on out," my great aunt informed me.

"Why is the preacher man putting sweet oil on their heads instead of in their ears?"

"That isn't sweet oil. It's olive oil, the purest of oils. Olives grow on evergreen trees. It's what the Bible says to use for anointing the sick when you pray a prayer of faith over them."

"Are you sure?" I wanted to believe but couldn't.

"I'm sure!"

"Why haven't I ever seen an olive tree growing and dripping oil in the Piney Woods before?" I asked.

My great aunt rolled her eyes way back into her head but didn't speak.

Nora woke up and looked over at us. She was interested in what we were saying. My heart stirred in my chest. I was afraid my chest would explode and leave me in a hundred or more pieces like the boy Jeremiah until I saw a piece of my heart jump out of my chest and head to Nora's chest. We smiled and became one in her pain. I clenched my chest, weak from sharing my strength with her.

"Nora, what happened to you?" I whispered to her.

"A train hit me," she whispered back to me.

"Great Aunt Annabelle, Nora was hit by a train!"

"Lord have mercy! Well, she's in the right place for a miracle to make her well!"

Looking at Nora, I was overcome with emotion. I didn't understand what was happening to me, let alone around me either. I felt like crying and running to Daddy and begging him to take me back to Meridian. I didn't because I felt like I had failed him and Momma too because of what I had written on my Prayer Ticket: L-i-f-e instead of asking the Lord for his healing.

The healing line was moving. We were almost next. Still, half the crowd was speaking in tongues throughout the tent as they waved their hands towards the sky while the other half danced.

Some folks were singing and clapping along with the choir who sang from *Amazing Grace.*

When we've been there ten thou-sand years, / Bright shining as the sun; / We've no less days to sing God's praise, / Than when we first be-gun.

I shivered and watched the folks' spirits separate from their bodies when the cloud passed over them while voices of every color continued to fill the night air with flicking flames of fire. When I looked into their faces, I saw a glow like our coal-oil lamp had when we lit it before a thunderstorm. Out of their mouths came an illumination into a night as dark as a field that had been burnt for the next year's harvest.

"Why in the world are those folks acting in such a way for? Are they from the Piney Woods bunch or what? Are they drinking moonshine whiskey?" I asked.

"They are dancing in the spirit! Remember when I read you the

Bible story about David dancing before the Lord with all his might? That's what these folks are doing," she went on.

"Are they going to take off their clothes like David did?"

Pushing me forward in the line while covering my mouth with her hands, "*Great day in the morning!* You don't miss a thing, do you?" she asked.

I shrugged.

Nora was next.

I took in a deep breath while her folks told the preacher man something. He reached for the olive oil and took a dab and touched her on the head and said, "In Jezzz-us' name, I seek ah miracle. Devil, turn this child loose! Lu-ci-fer, turn her loose! Saaa-tan, I command you to leee-ah-eee her body RIGHT NOW!"

Nora hasn't got the devil in her just a bad fever from eating flying squirrels and running from a fast train I bet!

Nothing happened. Nora lay still on her wooden board stretched out before the crowd until she closed her eyes like she was going on back to sleep.

"This Indian child hasn't got the faith for Jezzz-us Christ of Nazareth to touch her body!" the preacher man told the crowd while her folks looked on. "Take her away! She can't be healed unless she believes Jezzz-us can heal her body. She's got to believe!" he cried out.

The cloud began to lift up from amongst the people and to float out of the tent.

Turning to my great aunt for comfort, I said, "I thought he said we were all the Lord's children, every shape, color, and form. Why is he acting that way?"

She looked down and shrugged her shoulders.

Nora's too sick to even think. Dear God, please deliver Nora.

I didn't know what to do next.

When her folks began to take her away, I so wanted to run and tell her I would be her friend. But I didn't. All I was able to do was watch the Indian girl and feel my heart break to bits when she took her last breath and rolled off the board into some pine straw. Her momma let out a scream. Her daddy took her into his arms and carried her limp, lifeless shell of a body out of the selfsame side of the tent the cloud had left from as the elders looked on.

After what I'd witnessed, I had a feeling I would never be the same again the second the preacher man said to my Great Aunt Annabelle, "Sister, bring that little girl right on up here."

What to do now but go on!

I felt the feeling of faith, the power within me to believe, leave me. I wondered why a man of the Lord had treated an Indian girl like a bug. I looked down at my dress and saw the artificial paper marigold Opal had pinned near my heart for good luck. I took a deep breath and stepped forward, faithless as an empty Coca-Cola bottle.

The choir sang: *Jes-us, / O Je-sus, our holy Lord and Savior / Jes-us, without You we can't take a breath / You are our holy Lord and Savior / You know us each by name,* / Je-sus, / O, Je-sus how we pra-ise Your holy, bless-ed name, / Your bless-ed holy name / Je-sus, / O, Je-sus, we praise Your holy, bless-ed name.

The preacher man motioned for one of the elders to bring him a chair. He sat the chair in the center of the stage so everyone could see it. With a wave he said, "Little girl, come right on up here."

I turned to my great aunt for direction, and she nodded to go on.

I took another deep breath wishing I were back in my seat with my folks before walking onto the stage feeling more alone by the second. The preacher man never even asked me *why* I had come to the Salem Camp Meeting or even *what* or *if* I even wanted to be healed of anything. He made a motion with his hand for me to sit in the chair.

So, I did.

"This child has got a bad leg. Why it's *deformed! She's got a curse on her!*" he shouted out to the crowd and stretched both my legs straight in the front of me. He held my ankles while measuring my legs yet eyeing my second-hand red knee socks.

What's deformed?

I was too afraid to speak because he had the crowd's full attention. I knew every eye was on us. I looked around the tent and saw everyone was hanging onto his every word. All awaited his next move.

Listen, a voice spoke to my heart.

I watched him closely realizing unless I got healed, I wouldn't matter to him anymore than Nora did. That's when I knew I had better cooperate if I wanted to get out of the tent alive unlike dead Nora. Otherwise, I'd never get to go to school or see my folks again because I'd soon be dead and in the ground.

He cried out, "This child's left leg is about an inch or so shorter than her right leg is. The Lord God is going to heal her of her deformed leg! GLORY! I SAID GLORY to the Lord God!"

What's he talking about?

But sure enough, the way he was stretching my legs out in the front of me, he made the left one *seem* to look shorter than the right one.

"DON'T BE AFRAID OF THE LORD GOD'S POWER!" he

shouted to me.

"I AIN'T!" I shouted back, hoping for a chance to speak.

"Saints of God, sing it!" he cried out and blessed the choir then crowd with holy hand waves.

The choir along with the crowd sang: *He touched me and thus made me whole; / Bringing comfort and rest to my soul; / O glad, happy day, / all my sins rolled away! / For He touched me and thus made me whole.*

"Look at this poor child. She can't even walk straight I bet. Can you even run and play with the other children at school?" he asked.

"Why, no, because I've never got," I began, but he didn't let me finish.

"*Tch, tch, tch,* did you all hear her? She ain't never got to run and play with the other children at school!" he told the crowd.

"Bless her heart," said a kind voice.

"Would you look at her?" another voice instructed.

"She is filled with the pure faith of a child!" a woman's voice cried out.

"She sure is tall," a man marveled.

"Help her, Jesus," someone cried out.

"Sins of the father, sins of the father..." a voice observed.

"Ain't she a brave child!" another voice cried out.

"It's a manifestation of a pure curse!" said a man with a throaty, deep voice.

This is one time I'm glad my daddy can't hear!

I started to feel confounded when the choir began to sing O, *Why Not Tonight?*

"Don't you worry nary a bit because we are going to pray for the Lord God to touch your body and heal you of this here deformity the devil had done gone and put on your leg with a curse from the pit of hell! Yes, the Lord God is going to touch you," the preacher man told me while reaching for the sweet oil or olive oil or whatever it was, he was using.

I'm glad I'm sitting down so I won't fall out like those other folks did!

I tried hard to be thankful for something. It was hard because at that moment I felt like a mule.

He took a dab of the oil and then touched it on the top of my left foot and instructed me, "Tell us your first name."

"Mary."

The crowd roared, and with a face as red as fire, the preacher man grasped at his shirt and seized his necktie before announcing, "It's *HER!*"

"Holyholyholy, blessed be Jesus! The son of God. Holyholyholy, blessed be the Virgin Mary who gave Him life!" they began chanting.

My mind whirled.

Where's Great Aunt Annabelle? It was her old family letter from Rossville, Tennessee, that gave us the idea to come here anyhow. Now she's done gone and left me here all by myself with a pure stranger calling me by my first name that I never even think of unless someone asks me. And I don't even go to school!

Holding my legs straight out in front of me while eyeing my second-hand red knee socks, the preacher man yelled, "In Jezzz-us' name I seek ah miracle! In Jezzz-us' name, I said, grow. GROW! There it goes. Yes, there it goes! Can you see it growing? Look, *look!* There is goes. Yes, there it goes. Oh, my God! It's GROWING. Yes, it is!"

I looked down at my left leg.

"Did you see it grow?" the preacher man asked me.

All I saw was one of my new second-hand red knee socks that we had bought at the boiled peanut roadside stand on my left leg starting to *maybe* stretch a tiny bit right below my kneecap. So, because I saw that happen, I nodded.

The preacher man began yelling, "She's healed! Praise His

precious name! She SEEN it herself! Didn't you? Didn't you? Well, tell them. Don't be afraid, MARY. Speak up for Jezzz-uuu-sss! The Master has reached down from heaven and touched YOU, MARY! Without a doubt, the curse of the devil from the sins of your father and mother has been lifted straight ways up off you and been put under the throne of the Lord God Almighty in heaven!"

I looked down at my legs, unsure of what had happened, let alone if my leg had grown so much as a hair. "I saw my red sock move is all, but the real reason I come here was,"

"See? Mary saw the Lord God's power touch her leg when I prayed for her!" he went on, cutting my words off.

I was trying to remember when the Devil had cursed me on account of a sin that Momma and Daddy had committed. I was truly sorry for not asking the Lord for Daddy's healing. I wanted a second chance to make good on Momma's deal that saved my life at birth.

"HALLELUJAH, HALLELUJAH, and HALLELUJAH! he screamed out into the Salem Camp Meeting's crowd.

The choir rang out: O, why not tonight? / *Oh, why not tonight? / Wilt thou be saved? / Then, oh, yes why not tonight?*

He pulled me up so fast that I didn't have time to think what was happening before telling me to walk normal-like across the stage in front of the crowd. I walked as normal as I had ever walked while they all cheered me on.

"Glory Hallelujah!" someone cried out.

"But for the Cross!" a man shouted.

"The Power fell!" a voice cried out.

"JesusJesusJesus!" a young man yelled out, all excited about nothing and ran up to the side of the stage. He ran over to the open fire where the lighted torches were. He commenced to stick his naked hand straight into the orange-blue flames of fire and brought out the end that was glowing like an amber rose. I knew he was going to set fire to the tent, and we'd all wake up in a burning hell.

"The Power fell!" a voice cried out.

A group of folks began to dance all about the tent and shout and sing.

A woman with a potato figure and stark white hair began to laugh and laugh and laugh while she pranced up-and-down the aisles like an eight-point buck deer. After a while, she grabbed hold of a little baby and began cradling it while laughing like a hyena. The baby never cried one tear. I thought that it must be dead, and I was going to die too if somebody didn't do something quick to help me get off the stage and get myself on back home to Meridian.

Dear Lord God, please help me get out of this tent alive! I'm sorry for writing L-i-f-e on my bonafide Prayer Ticket. Please, help me!

Half the crowd held hands and began to sway back and forth. The music roared like the wind all through the tent. I thought my ear drums had burst because for one minute or maybe even two, I couldn't hear a thing.

Now I'm deaf like Daddy!

Somehow, I managed to turn and look towards the side of the tent where the very same young fellow who had grabbed hold of the blazing torch had taken to running. I watched him run like he'd been struck by a bolt of lightning about five or six times around the tent until he came upon a pole that held a basketball goal and net. He ran not around it but straight up it like it was nothing more than an out-of-place sidewalk around a house in a big city.

I'm in trouble now!

The preacher man took to blowing on the conch shell like no tomorrow was coming. To my mind, the elders seemed to be growing taller by the minute. The louder he blew on his conch shell, the more I felt like David without a sling to slay Goliath. I felt naked but not dancing like David was known to do before the Lord my God with the giant elders approaching me. Why, I didn't know. I shut my eyes and prayed to disappear. But I didn't disappear.

When I opened them again, I felt far worse at that very second than I had ever felt before. I felt darkness instead of light in the moment. I felt alone too. I didn't have the heart to tell them I didn't come for my leg to grow. Besides, I wasn't sure if it had grown or not, truth be told. I had no idea who had put a curse on me either. I began to wonder if all the other things I had seen were real or not. The preacher man was confusing me and making me doubt my own self-worth even more so than I already did, not to mention what I had seen with my own two eyes and felt inside my heart. I knew right then and there I had failed not only my folks but the Lord too all because I wanted a good life with friends and family and all that other folks I'd seen have and I didn't.

What to do?

My Great Aunt Annabelle walked up and grabbed me by the hand and led me off the stage without saying so much as a single word. I was so glad to see her that I didn't even look back nor did I thank the preacher man for whatever *he thought* he had done for me in Jesus' name.

"Myra, why didn't you tell me you had a deformed leg?" she asked, walking faster by the minute.

"What's deformed?" I asked, trying to keep up.

"Damaged or marred. Your left leg isn't perfect!"

"I didn't know my left leg wasn't perfect. Daddy says I'm perfect in every way."

"It must have been twisted at birth!"

"I was a breech baby."

"Well, that explains it!"

"How did I get a curse on me? Is that why I can't go to school?"

"Sweet Jesus! How would I know?" She walked faster.

"I thought I had enough faith to please the Lord. Great Aunt Annabelle, why are you acting mad at me for?"

"Listen Myra, I'm not mad, so to speak. I'm disappointed that you didn't tell the preacher man what you came here for!"

"Well, it isn't my fault. I tried to tell him, but he wouldn't listen to me. Why did he ask for my first name anyway? I was afraid I was going to die like the others did!"

"No one died any more than Virgil got a healing from his deafness! To get a healing is why we came, right?" She jerked her neck so hard that I heard it pop.

"Well, he can get healed at the house as well. I bet you a dollar he can."

She didn't answer. Instead, she walked ahead into the crowd like she had forgotten who I was, or something far worse like she was ashamed of me.

I saw my folks who had been joined by Opal and Eddy all waiting for us by the drinking well beside the 23rd tent. The pure relief that filled my heart when I caught sight of them gave me such joy that I wanted to explode.

One of them must have told my daddy what was said and what had happened up on the stage with the chair because he was standing there waiting for me with his arms open wide. He shouted, "Bay-bay-do-do-lll, ca-ca-ca-ho-ho-ho-mmm-tah me!"

I obliged him.

Momma asked, "What in the world did that preacher man do to my baby girl?"

Everyone eyed my legs.

"He didn't do a thing to me nor did the Lord. Well, not that I know of anyway," I told them, feeling relieved to be back with them.

"Miss Myra, is your leg well or ain't it?" Eddy asked, Opal close by his side.

"Where in Sam Hill have you two been?" I asked them.

"We had to sit in the back of the healing tent 'cause we is Colored folks and ain't fit to sit up in the front with the white folks," Opal blurted out.

"That's a lie from the devil, if they is one," I started to say. Daddy put his hand over my mouth to stop me from speaking.

Eddy whispered, "Child, now you best hush up 'afore somebody loads up in a truck full of Ku Klux Klan men and comes on out to tha house in Meridian and causes you and your'n folks a heavy heap of trouble."

"Momma, what does he mean? And why is Great Aunt Annabelle acting mad at me for? Did the Indian girl, Nora, die? What about the baby with the dancing lady? Was it dead or alive? Is Daddy healed?"

"Myra, Aunt Annabelle isn't mad. She loves you too much. That's all," was all she said to me. Suddenly, I believed maybe the Lord had had mercy on me and healed Daddy anyway. For a minute or two, I thought maybe I hadn't failed them after all, and we'd soon have a good life.

I looked over towards the 23rd tent and saw a stark, white-headed, lion-like man eyeing us. When his eyes caught mine, he put his middle finger in the center of his nose and pushed it hard like he was crushing it, an old sign for Negro or Colored in the South.

Daddy spelled out, "L-e-t'-s g-o," and looked away.

I whispered, "Daddy, I love you," to see if he could hear me. No words came. Not even a glance. That's when I knew for sure I had not only failed the Lord my God by not having the faith to believe and speak up to the preacher man, but I'd also failed to simply do what was right and true by my folks—make good on Momma's promise to the Lord who had given me life in the first place. I was confused. My faith was shaken.

We headed for The Rainbow with me bouncing on Daddy's hip while he did his best to miss the potholes. I looked back to see if I could get another glimpse of Nora, but neither she nor her folks were anywhere in sight.

Someone cried out, "N-lovers! N-lovers!"

And what followed were showers of fresh eggs amid more cries of "N-lovers! Retards! White trash! Git on back home!"

When Daddy and Eddy went back to fight what looked like a gang of boys not yet men, it was Momma who ran and stood in front of Daddy and cried out, "The Bible says, turn the other cheek. Leave vengeance to the Lord! Virgil, let them be!"

Strangely enough, neither Daddy nor Eddy fought back. However, Daddy got so mad he took the oyster jar of moonshine whiskey he'd hidden in his sock out and threw it into the corner of The Rainbow's flatbed where it smashed and filled the back of the truck with smelly liquor.

I don't know what was worse, an unexpected egging, words filled with hate, or that two grown men were unable to defend themselves for fear of the Lord their God. It was all sad to watch. Real sad.

In the flatbed of The Rainbow, Momma covered me with her lap blanket and lay down beside me, and together we cried, softly. I don't mind telling you. I wanted to die. I believe a part of me did die on the inside of the Salem Camp Meeting. Then, when I realized the eyes of my heart were no longer flooded with hope for my prayers to be answered about anything. I had no desire to even speak amid the smell of fresh eggs and moonshine whiskey.

My spirit took me to a deep place to survive my confusion. I was too young to understand what had happened in the name of Christian love that Halloween night. And as if the Lord was crying too, the dark skies of that October night opened with the gift of rain over The Rainbow. Watching the rain fall on my face, I considered what I had printed on my bonafide Prayer Ticket *L-i-f-e*.

The Lord had given me what I'd prayed for, yet my life would never be the same again. I felt broken and slammed to pieces. I knew I would never have a good life. I felt for the artificial paper marigold pinned on my dress, pulled it off, and saw that it was unrecognizable. I threw it from The Rainbow like the poor white trash most people thought we were.

Save for Momma's over-flowing tears, the rest of us remained silent and packed like sardines in the oblong truck bed of The Rainbow. An October rain redeemed us of the sins of the Salem Camp Meeting while we rode back to Meridian as empty and as sad as ever.

L-I-F-E BY LOVE, FIRE, AND LIGHT

Chapter 6

December 18, 1961

LIKE WITH many things that didn't make good sense in our family, not another word was said about the Salem Camp Meeting, Daddy not getting a healing, if Nora or the baby had died, or our being cursed as n-lovers, white trash, or retards let alone if my leg had grown or not. We acted like that night at the Salem Camp Meeting had never happened at all. It was around Christmastime, when one night after I had settled into bed with Kitty Momma, I heard Daddy cry out with enough moonshine whiskey in him to make him remember what we had pretended to forget.

"Ga-ga-ga ha-da-da-mi-mi-mi-ti-ti-ti-it sun--sun-sun-na-na-na-fa-fa-fa-ba-ba-ba-ch-it! Na-na-na-ot go-na-na-na ga-ga-ga-it ah-way wi-th ha-ha-ha 'mule-at-ing mi ba-ba-ba-yyy do-do-do-lll!"

"Now Virgil," Momma began. Her words were like drops of rain falling into a cast iron hot skillet amid Daddy's drunken anger. "Virgil, you can't do anything more. You got to leave vengeance to the Lord. The Bible says, "Vengeance is mine, saith the Lord. I will repay... Yes, the Lord will repay them!"

Daddy turned wild and screamed, "U-U-U-! Bibibi-lll-lll-lll-ee-ee-ee n-n-n hh-hh-hh-ee-ee-ee-lll-lll-lll!"

I heard Momma scream, "NO! Virgil Boone, you give me the butcher knife!"

"U-U-U!"

I could hear my folks running through the house. I thought I was safe behind a locked door from the demon that comes with moonshine whiskey, the one who can make a man do bad things to the ones he loves most, but I was wrong. I was horrified watching the blade of a butcher knife break through the wood of my bedroom door. The wild man, the one as mean as a starving summer rattlesnake who had taken over Daddy's body, made me wish I could disappear. Shivering, crying, and holding onto Kitty Momma, I counted the blade's blows. It was seven in all.

Momma screamed, "*In the name of Jesus, Devil, leave this house!*"

Oh, no! The Devil followed us back to Meridian and has hold of Daddy!

After what felt like an eternal silence, Momma cried out, "I plead the blood of Jesus! Devil, leave this house NOW!"

Great Aunt Annabelle sleeps like a rock!

I knew it was only me and Kitty Momma to hear the devil in Daddy until I heard him relent to muffled cursing sounds against the backdrop of Momma's tears. Filled with fear and scared to breathe, I searched my mind once again for where the Lord was. I had been so hopeful, so filled with faith that the Salem Camp Meeting was going to be a means to my end of sadness. Instead, all my hopes and dreams were dashed, shattered like broken glass because I was witnessing everybody I loved in the world go stark raving mad and turn on one another like a starving pack of stray dogs. Again, the next morning everyone pretended like nothing had happened, but it wasn't as easy as it had always been over the years when Daddy had thrown a drunk.

No matter how hard we pretended, none of us could ignore the seven holes in my bedroom door made by an earthly devil holding a moonshine whiskey-driven butcher knife in his hand, a hand like mine, empty of hopes and dreams.

Like always, Daddy promised us to stop his drinking. But like Momma had said, that is one promise no man, dead or alive, no man can keep for long, save for taking hold of the Lord's healing hand. Something even I had been unable to do was take hold of the Lord's healing hand because I had trusted in my own two hands and written *L-i-f-e* on my bonafide prayer ticket.

COME ONE WEEK BEFORE CHRISTMAS, December 18, to be exact, the men folk, Daddy, and Eddy, screened some of the windows while the women, Momma, Opal, Great Aunt Annabelle, and me, shared a bag of Hershey Kisses and tall glasses of cold water. Kitty Momma even got a rolled-up ball of silver paper to paw around on the front porch.

Daddy had kept his promise for a few weeks to lay off the whiskey. And his way of saying *I'm sorry* for showing out and stabbing my door with a butcher knife was to make my bedroom look like a doll house until we could save enough money for a new door. He'd special-ordered a tiny window and a screen from Reynolds' Mercantile so when him and Eddy came home from carpentering, they could put me in a little window over the front door to look out with Kitty Momma. They cut out the hole and put it in after a hard day's work. It was beautiful. It took away some of my sadness too like pretty things can often do for a body.

In the cool evening of the same December day, we found ourselves in the front yard sitting under the pecan trees telling stories to pass the time. Then, with Daddy watching Momma's lips, she turned and asked me, "Myra, did I ever tell you how your daddy started to court me and how we fell in love?"

"No."

He turned to her and signed three times, "I love you."

"A-hold your horses a doggone minute. I want to hear this love story!" Great Aunt Annabelle cried out, pulling up an old oak rocker we had found on the side of the road in a ditch. Opal and Eddy each took a seat in store-bought rocker on the porch by the front door.

"Over in Goodlife, Momma and Poppa Davis had invited all the families in the community over to Magnolia Sunday to listen to the Grand Ole Opry on our radio and sit under the pecan trees one Saturday night. Virgil came to listen to the Opry for some notable sound of his once best friend, Ray Charles. While everyone else danced, we slipped off to the back yard and snuck in a dance," Momma told us.

Opal moved in closer to Eddy.

Momma turned and asked Daddy, "Remember?"

"Yah ba-ba-ba-ttt!" he rang out.

"Why did they call it Magnolia Sunday?" I asked her.

"In early 1900, after my Momma and Poppa Davis were first married, they were returning home one bright Sunday afternoon from their Capitol weekend honeymoon in Jackson. When their tires hit the driveway, the first tree they saw in full bloom was a magnolia tree. So, they decided to name the Davis home place *Magnolia* to celebrate their new life together and *Sunday* for their first day on the farm as man and wife," she told me.

Smiling, I listened on.

Eddy said, "I'll be damn. Leave it to white folks to write poetry about a dumb house and a big tree on Sunday."

Momma turned and gave him a look he wouldn't soon forget.

Opal frogged his arm.

"Owl-weee!" Eddy screamed out.

Kitty Momma jumped up into Great Aunt Annabelle's lap. She was rocking away like no tomorrow was a-coming.

Opal and Eddy moved to the front porch steps to drink in every word of love filling the December night air.

"O-pa-lll, git icicic-d tea?" Daddy turned and asked her.

"Sure will," Opal turned and said to him.

"And I'll get the mint," I said, heading for the mint bed.

Momma waited for Opal to get the iced tea and me to return with the mint to finish her story of love.

"Anyway," she began.

Daddy butted in. "My-gold, 'bout mah hahaha-at," he said, smiling all the while.

Momma turned and said to him, "Virgil, if you will let me tell it my way, I'll get to it."

He grinned and shrugged his shoulders at everyone. Turning back toward her, "Ssasasa-uit, yayaya-sasa-f, the-n," he said.

My daddy doesn't get his feelings hurt by anyone!

It was as hard for him as it was for the rest of us when he talked, but no matter what he said or how he said it, I loved him with all my heart. I knew that I would always be his *Bay-doll* and Momma would always be his *My-gold.*

"I want to hear about the Grand Ole Opry," Great Aunt Annabelle said, adding a sprig of mint to her iced tea.

Momma went on with, "Myra, like I was saying, we had slipped off by ourselves to the backyard to dance. Well, I want you to know Virgil Boone was the most handsome man in the Union Community. I thought his light brown, sun-kissed skin was firm, strong, and beautiful kind of like when you unwrap a Hershey Kiss."

I laughed.

"He still is right good-looking," Great Aunt Annabelle turned and said to him.

"T-h-a-n-k y-o-u," Daddy spelled, giving her a thumb up.

Everyone laughed.

"Once, I danced with Virgil, that's when he started to court me. Of course, we kept it to ourselves," she said.

"Rarara-ite-n-her-eee-er," Daddy cut in, laughing and shaking his head.

"That's right nice, ain't it?" Opal said.

"Yep. It sho' enough sounds romantic enough for me," Eddy agreed before shouting, "Woo-hoo! Opal and me love to dance by ourselves juds't the same. 'Though we ain't never danced under a tree before."

Laughing while clapping his hands, Daddy spelled out, "Y-e-a-h b-o-y!" and gave me a sky-high wave.

I waved back.

"Kind of nice, I thank," Opal said dreamily.

"Yes, it was. The problem was that we had to keep sneaking, meeting and then pretending to go to the outhouse. We went behind a fig tree to dance and dance and dance, not under the pecan trees like everybody else. I told him about my teaching Sunday School in Goodlife. I remember he smelled of Wrigley's Juicy Fruit gum, not moonshine whiskey like he does nowadays."

"Hahaha-at," Daddy blurted out like a small child and pointed to his head.

"Myra, your daddy has always been known for having the finest hats around. That night he was sporting a John B. Stetson Calvary hat. He and Brother Ray had worked at a Saint Augustine charity home for deaf and blind boys making fine crafts and selling them once a year at the Florida State Fair. He told me he had saved up for a year and mail ordered his hat from Philadelphia, Pennsylvania. They were a pair of monkeys in a barrel all right, always funning and cutting up—Ray and his blindness and your daddy and his deafness. Ray was always singing and Virgil dancing when they were together like neither of them had a care in the world. They were close friends from way back. To them, white was black and black was white—both one and the same. But Myra, not everybody thought like them. And they never will."

"Two Tom cats a-catin' around town! I'd bet you a dollar that's what they were doing," Great Aunt Annabelle said, clapping her hands in front of her.

"Ray Charles can sho'nough carry ah tune, can't he?" Eddy cut in.

"I know Ray be right proud to have a voice to help him make it outta the South," Opal turned and said towards the cool of the night air.

"That Elvis Presley boy made it out of Mississippi too by shaking his legs," my great aunt said, looking at a full December moon that was rising while the day's sun snuck out of sight.

Opal got up and went and turned on the front porch light.

"Rrr-ray mmm-yyy," Daddy said then spelled, "b-e-s-t f-r-i-e-n-d."

Momma butted in with, "Virgil, wasn't Ray the best basket weaver the home for boys ever tuned out, not to mention the way he taught himself to figure musical notes the hard way by counting them out one by one in his head?"

"Ye-e-s, My-gold," he spelled and clapped his hands once.

"My Virgil was a real handsome man back then. Ray wasn't as good-looking as he is nowadays. He was too skinny if you ask me. Now folks always said Virgil's face had a glow of truth about it," she mused, then added, "and somehow Ray Charles saw it too."

"You wuz took with him. That wuz it. Plum took," Opal said before she blurted out, "Like bacon and grits!"

"I'd say you wuz in tall cotton for s'hore," Eddy said, shaking his head while grinning like a spider monkey.

"I was willing myself for true love for certain," Momma said, smiling.

I noticed when Daddy took a gulp from his tea glass, he began to drool.

"Virgil teased me for the longest time that it was 'love at first sight,'" she said, turning toward Daddy who flipped his right hand her way.

"Nothin' be wrong with that," Eddy said, forgetting to turn toward Daddy.

"Virgil told me if he ever got to California that he was going to ask Ray to write a song about our story of love, didn't you?" Momma turned and asked Daddy, but instead of answering her, he reached into his pocket for a handkerchief and wiped the slobber from his chin.

Without any warning, I saw a man appear in the form of a yellow-flamed sun, jam-packed with eyes shining with a crystal blue-orange fire. He was holding a double-edged sword between my folks.

"I l-o-v-e, l-o-v-e, l-o-v-e, l-o-v-e, y-o-u," Daddy turned and spelled four times before sitting his empty iced tea glass down.

"I l-o-v-e y-o-u t-h-e m-o-s-t," Momma, who was already facing him, spelled back.

Daddy and Eddy got up and went into the Piney Woods behind the house and soon came back with a loblolly pine tree. It would serve as our Christmas tree. Daddy said maybe we could put it up the next day.

For some reason, I remembered back to spring when the night wind would join us and stir a cool breeze through the tops of the mimosa trees until they made little pink and white silk whispers above our heads and the hundreds of light bugs that would ride in on the night wind. When I would turn to see if I could catch a tail-end glimpse of the wind before it left, I would only see the tiny lightning bugs blinking green flashes to the early dark of the evening. But that would never happen in the cool of December.

When I looked to see what Great Aunt Annabelle and Kitty Momma had to say about the story of love, all I saw were two gray shadows fast asleep in the moon's glow. When Momma and Daddy said goodnight, I saw the man in the form of a yellow-flamed sun disappear as fast as he had appeared. Opal and Eddy understood the time-to-go signs and left for Quitman.

LATER ON, into the night, Kitty Momma woke me up licking at my neck. I figured she wanted me to get up and let her out so she could join Daddy boiling his midnight coffee to cover up his late-night drinking. After sleepily observing the air was still and without the smell of boiling coffee, I drifted on back to sleep. The next time I opened my eyes, I saw the room was filling with a cloud like the one I saw the night I met Nora at the tent meeting. Only this time the cloud was red and lined with red-orange fire. When I sat up, my ears began to ring while my nose burned with the smell of sulfur. My bedroom was overcome with lights dazzling like sunbeams.

I saw a man who was eight feet tall setting his eyes straight on me amid a great wave of confusion that began to move all about the room when a giant bird with the face and form of a man joined the tall man. They were friends. Startled and shaken with icy fear, I watched the beings' faces light the walls of my bedroom with a red-orange hue. As fast as fear had overtaken me, I felt it leave when, with a voice like a song, they spoke words from many languages that I did not understand showing me, as fast as time, glimpses of worlds I did not know existed.

I felt my confusion turn to compassion when the voice wrapped itself around the table of my heart and opened my understanding by dropping one word into my mind: *Believe*.

As if the universe were sympathetic to the moment, their wings stirred, and in panorama I was shown the lighted story of my life from its conception to its ultimate transcendence. Then, in a sudden transforming wave of power too profound to comprehend, the sunbeam visitors and I became one light.

My bedroom window shot open.

"What do you want me to do?" I asked the light now inside me.

No answer.

Smoke took my breath. Kitty Momma was pacing the floor beneath the open window. I felt a new strength enter my body. My sadness left. In the blink of an eye, I snatched Kitty Momma and jumped through the window into the darkness of the Piney Woods. I saw my mind running far ahead of me, and hundreds of tiny green, squared pictures flashed before my eyes until I tripped and fell on my face. When I stood to my feet, I realized I had run off without my folks, so I turned and headed back to the house where the night air reeked with an unidentifiable odor. The smell grew thicker and thicker, so thick I could taste it in the roof of my mouth.

Like an animal, I crawled on my belly into the living room where

I saw the gas heater was blazing, and tiny embers were spitting bits of paper sparkles through its vents. Intuitively, I reached into the sparkling embers as parts of the roof began to fall.

Great Aunt Annabelle and Momma ran into the living room screaming. Their night gowns on fire. Yet, when Momma saw me, she stopped and gathered me into her arms. We three would have made it out the front door except that I began to scream, "*Nooooooo!* Get Daddy! He can't hear the fire burning!"

Momma got confused and stumbled, but she managed to throw me out the front door. As I rolled out of her arms, down the front steps, somehow, I got caught up in the Loblolly pine that was to be our Christmas tree. Together, the Christmas tree and I rolled out into the yard where I saw Great Aunt Annabelle rolling around in the dirt to put her night gown out. When I lifted my head, I saw Momma give me a stricken, decisive look of love that I read as a goodbye. I felt my spirit break when I watched her run back into the burning house with my great aunt close behind her.

After I got myself untangled from the now useless Christmas tree, I turned to see the roof collapse and bury alive the only three people that I had ever loved in the entire world. I cried and rocked and held myself until after a while, I turned myself loose, becoming aware the fingers on my hands were numb. When I looked at my hands, I saw my right was burned and festering like bacon frying in a cast iron skillet on the eye of a hot stove. My left hand was scorched and unrecognizable.

Oh, no! What to do now?

My senses were numb, yet somehow my eyes were drawn back into the fire where I saw three clouds forming within its dancing purple, orange, and blue flames. Three apparitions rose from the flames and floated over the house before disappearing into the starry December's night sky. Once again, the stench of the unidentifiable odor filled my lungs and overpowered me.

When I tasted death, I began to vomit and vomit and vomit until there was a blessed, welcomed loss of awareness as an extraordinarily strong disgust too immense for human consciousness moved into my stomach. I blacked out.

THE OPPORTUNITY HOUSE

Chapter 7

December 19, 1961

WHEN I WOKE UP, five were girls staring at me like I was a diamond ring.

"My name is Elisha Pearl," said a Colored girl.

"I am P-a-u-l-a," spelled another who then said, "Paul-ah."

"You got any Hershey Kisses?" asked one of the girls.

I blinked, sat up, and began to rock. I looked around the room and my eyes stopped on a little robin-egg blue cardboard plaque with a silver glitter inscription that read: *Faith can break the sky in two and let the face of God shine through.*

The smallest of the five announced, "This here's Susie, La-nette, but we call her Net. I am Faith. And, you, Girly Girl, are in the Opportunity House."

My pain was too great for words, so I closed my eyes and went back to sleep. When I awoke again, the five girls were still staring at me.

It was the smallest girl, Faith, who spoke first. "Who you?"

Don't talk! an unfamiliar voice said to my heart.

I didn't answer her. Instead, I blinked.

Paula came to my defense by saying, "Faith, let her alone. If she hasn't anything to say right now, then she ain't talky."

Faith flung her a sharp look. A small dachshund joined us. He sat up on his haunches and smiled at me.

"This here's Lucy," Net said.

Lucy barked and pointed like a bird dog.

"Lucy likes to hunt rats better than any cat I've ever seen," Paula told me.

"Hush! You'll scare her," Net said.

Lucy barked, "*Ah, ruff! Ah, ruff!*"

I looked at my hands and saw two cotton knee socks secured at each wrist by rubber bands. Memories of rainbow-like flames began to flash in my mind. My thoughts filled with flashes of black and white pictures along with hot, yet icy, screams and I remembered the fire.

Where is Momma, Daddy, Great Aunt Annabelle, and Kitty Momma?

Tears streamed down my face when I became aware that my fingers had no feeling. My heart jumped then shook me when I remembered what I wanted to forget. My remembering pain was great.

"*Ah, ruff! Ah, ruff! Ah, ruff!*" Lucy barked on.

Again, I began to rock. I tried to wipe my eyes but boxed myself instead with the cotton socks.

Paula patted my shoulder. "There, there, there. You have come at the perfect time."

"Calm yourself down," Faith blurted out while pinching her cheeks.

I blinked.

What's wrong with me?

I tried to bite through the rubber bands. *I hate socks!*

I remembered my second-hand red socks and the trouble they had caused me at the Salem Camp Meeting.

"Stop! If Mr. Moloch or his old lady sees you, you'll get it no matter what fix you're in!" Susie screamed.

"Hush! Don't scare her. I said, hush!" Net ordered her, fanning the air.

"Looks like we'll call her, Girly Girl, until her name comes up," Faith said with a shrug.

"*Girly Girl?* What kind of a name is *that?*" Paula asked.

Reaching for Lucy, Susie asked, "I don't know. Do you, Lucy?"

"Welcome to the Opportunity House, Girly Girl," Faith said.

Lucy rolled her big, sad eyes around then to me and barked, "*Ah, ruff! Ah, ruff!*"

I felt sick to my stomach.

"We all kin folk here. Yep. But not blood kin. We kin on account of not having anybody but each other. Nobody gives a damn about nary a one of us," Elisha Pearl blurted out.

The others nodded in agreement.

Susie set Lucy down on the floor and ordered, "Go catch me another varmint!"

"*Ah, ruff!*" Lucy barked and ran out of the room.

Paula gave me a kind look and said, "She's not up to talking yet.

Leave her be."

One look at my cotton socks wrapped hands left me lost for words.

"Would you like a cool drink of water?" Net asked me.

I nodded not knowing what else to do.

Susie spoke up, "Let me get it," then turned and ran out of the same door Lucy had taken.

"Girly Girl, can you talk or not?" Net asked me.

I nodded.

"Maybe we should put some leeches on her," Elisha Pearl said, reaching behind her for an old stone circular pot. She reached in and brought back a chubby worm for me to see. Smiling, she flicked the worm back into the stone pot before putting it back on a shelf.

"What in the name of God do you mean scaring her like that?" Faith asked.

"I saw a picture of leeches in *Cures of Old*," Elisha Pearl went on to say, shrugging her shoulders at the others and looking serious when she added, "That's how I learned about bleeding a body. Ain't got no momma or no poppa to teach me nary a thing! How else will I learn if I don't look at picture books?"

I frowned, feeling my cheeks burn.

"Nobody in this room needs a *leech!* Stop with your'n foolishness!"

Faith shouted.

Elisha Pearl threw her a hurt look. Paula ran over and gave her half a hug. Lucy entered the room like a streak of lightning with her toenails clicking on the wood floor.

Susie gave me a nice taste of ice water.

"Sweet Jesus!" Elisha Pearl said when she saw Lucy's jaws stuffed with a fat rat.

Susie left the room marveling, "Gosh, what a dog! What a dog! If she was bigger, I betcha we could teach her to fetch us a deer. Then, we wouldn't have to eat rats on white bread drowned in ketchup when we run out of food on some Saturdays!"

I frowned.

When Elisha Pearl saw me frown, she said, "Girly Girl, eatin' rats on white bread drowned in ketchup every once in a while, are bettern' than usin' your finger for a straw and eatin' your own vomit! I've been so hungry that I wanted to die to get shed of the pain of emptiness in my stomach. Don't you ever forget it was me who told you that either. Understand?"

I nodded.

Lucy sat beside the bed, and droplets of blood trickled on the floor from her catch.

"Not on our maple floor! It's the only pretty thing we got around here, 'sides Paula's almanac," Faith screamed out while holding her head.

"Nice catch, Lucy," Net said in an encouraging voice.

Lucy moved, and her toenails clicked on the maple floor before she barked, "*Ah, ruff! Ah, ruff! Ah, ruff!*"

"Girly Girl, Lucy likes you! See the big one she's fetched for you?" Net observed.

They don't have any books or toys!

Susie came back in and gave me another drink of water from a tin and announced, "I'm going to get my ears pierced as soon as I turn twenty-one."

I blinked.

"Jezebel!" Elisha Pearl shouted.

"Ain't neither!" Susie said.

Lucy moved back a little, gulping on the rat to secure it in her jaws. It splashed more blood on the floor.

"You are gonna to grow up to be like your whore of a momma!" Elisha Pearl cried out.

"Ain't neither!" Susie argued back at her.

"Both of you shut up!" Faith scolded them.

"Stupid! I hate you all!" Susie screamed, running towards a little door off to the side of the room.

"Girly Girl, if you got to pee or do number two, we got our own indoor toilet with a sink and running water. We got everything; even toilet paper so you don't have to use old newspaper," Net whispered to me.

I nodded.

"She ain't gonna ever say nothing I bet," someone whispered to Paula then added, "Maybe she's a *mute*."

What's a mute?

Susie ran back into the room wiping her hands on her skirt.

Someone cut in and said, "Will someone run and get an old shoe box so that we can bury this here varmint?"

"I got one in my closet," Susie said, heading for her closet.

When Lucy released her catch, Paula said, "Good job, Lucy."

Susie smiled and handed Paula an old shoe box.

I sized them up like five different doors waiting to be opened.

Paula was a slender, ageless blonde girl. Her dress was like an old quilt with its yellow, blue, pink scraps of material pieced together by red thread. A string of light blue beads dangled from her neck. All in all, she was as neat as a pin.

Susie, maybe thirteen, had strawberry blonde hair. She was draped in a light green old curtain of a shift dress. In her hair was a yellow ribbon that drooped over her eyes like a wilted sunflower.

Elisha Pearl, a big breasted, thick girl had smooth brown skin. Her thick jet-black glasses matched her snarled curly hair. She wore an orange print dress that had a gingerbread man with a crooked blue smile sewn near her heart. On her wrists someone had painted red, white, and blue flag-like bracelets. Red stars dotted her earlobes.

Faith, a perky soul and maybe ten, had on a pair of navy blue overalls with a crisp, white T-shirt with a tiny leather-like old red book stuffed inside her bib pocket. She looked like a little boy.

Net, a sophisticated girl for her young years, was dressed in the prettiest dress of all. It was robin-egg blue with white and vertical stripes. The initials *J. F. K.* were monogrammed in red near her waistline. She had on a thick navy blue belt even though she didn't need it.

While I was observing that everyone was barefooted, Net asked, "What is she looking at us like *that* for?"

Susie shrugged.

Faith blurted out, "Girly Girl, before we go and bury Lucy's catch, I want you to know before too long, we got to go and get Mr. Moloch and his old lady so they can come and take a look at you. You've been asleep for a long time. The Moloch's are the ones who run this here place. And I don't mind telling you that they are two of a kind!"

I nodded.

"They the ones we are beholding too, on account of giving us a place to stay," Susie said.

"They get pretty near one hundred dollars or maybe even more a month from the Relief man for the lot of us," Elisha Pearl announced, then whispered, "Stay away from Mr. Moloch unless one of us is with you." Winking at me, "He's a *rascal* who forces himself on us once we go to sleep. Said he'd kill us one by one if we tell it. We got Christmas plans for him; sugar cookies laced with rat poison. That's why we taught Lucy to hunt rats so we could stockpile the poison. Listen, we agreed that we'd rather eat the extra rats to get shed of him!" She took the rat from Lucy and put it in the old shoe box.

Faith left the room.

Paula said, "Girly Girl, Mr. Moloch can unwrap your hands."

I blinked, still unable to speak.

Susie kicked the shoe box and rat under the bed.

I nodded. I felt a throbbing in the tips of my fingers. I heard voices before Faith, a man, and a woman entered the room.

"Well, little lady," a deep throated, unsympathetic voice began. "I'm Mr. Moloch, and this here is my wife Mrs. Moloch. From what them two Coloreds who called the law this morning said, you must be Mary Myra Boone. Is that right?"

Mrs. Moloch walked over and gave me the once over casting a cloud of darkness when she moved about the room.

"She ain't able to talk. We ain't for sure if she's muted or not," Net told them.

In a marveling voice, Mrs. Moloch said, "Oh, my goodness! We've never had to look after a *mute* before." Her hair was pinned back with gray, greasy wisps hanging carefree and loose around her face.

Mr. Moloch looked at the others who were standing at attention and silent for the first time since I'd laid my eyes on them. He cupped the chin of his square face with one hand and reached into his pocket with the other and brought out a pair of scissors. His jagged, tobacco-colored teeth parted to let his rancid breath fill the room.

Mrs. Moloch moved closer to me and reached for my hands. I wondered why they didn't explain or talk to me to make me feel better. But they never did; in fact, they seemed to talk *at me* instead of *to me* like I was invisible.

Wide-eyed though silent, the girls watched the couple closely.

Mrs. Moloch spoke up and sharply said, "Mary, hold still while we unwrap your'n hands."

I nodded, even though being called Mary hurt me in a way I'd never been hurt before.

"*Auahahahaha! Auahahahaha!*" I screamed.

The girls jumped back when Mrs. Moloch pulled off the rubber bands. She moved onto the cotton socks, but Mr. Moloch got impatient with her and grabbed my hands and began ripping more than cutting the socks half in two.

When I began to cry and scream louder, Paula gave me a fearful look.

After a while, with what felt like purposeful cruelty from the Molochs' pulling and cutting and unwrapping, both cotton socks came off my hands.

"*Sweet Jesus!*" Mr. Moloch screamed, eyeing my hands.

When I looked down at my hands; I could not believe they even belonged to me. Both looked like raw deer steaks.

"*Auahahahaha! Auahahahaha!*" I continued to scream.

The girls gasped in unison.

While pushing greasy strands of hair back over his bulging bald forehead, Mr. Moloch shot them a mean look before saying, "Hell, this one is ruined for life!"

I moaned.

Mrs. Moloch told them, "You got that right! Mary is going to have to learn how to hold a pencil between her front teeth to even print her name. She'll grow up to be a retard."

"Maybe her nerves are bad like all of ours," Faith whispered to Paula.

Paula offered, "If she stays on, I'll be happy to look after her."

"I doubt she'll stay long because some of her people have been located over towards the city of Goodlife," Mrs. Moloch said.

"She's got *people*?" someone asked.

When I looked up, Paula smiled then nodded at me.

Even though there was something about Paula that comforted me, I still felt helpless, scared, and numb.

"Her people called, eh? When?" Mr. Moloch asked her.

What people?

With a laugh beneath her voice, Mrs. Moloch announced, "A Mister Spurgeon Davis did about an hour ago. He said he and his wife Reatha would be here as quick as they could to fetch her. Grandfolks from which side of the fence—the front or the back—I don't know."

I looked at the girls and almost at once all their faces dropped except for Paula who smiled at me.

I don't even know my people!

I felt my skin crawl when Mr. Moloch bent down and gave my cheek a soft but sure lick. He said, "Sweet Mary, now don't you worry if they don't fetch you because fresh meat is always welcome at the Opportunity House."

I didn't understand what he meant, but I knew it wasn't good.

After the Molochs put clean bandages on my hands and left, Faith walked over and whispered, "You must escape before he does to you what he's done to us. It's too ugly to talk about. I can promise you this: There is no *opportunity* in the Opportunity House. It's only a name to fool folks into giving their money away like many hardshells, lying preachers fool folks into doing in their Jesus-believing worlds."

Paula started patting me once again.

Susie said, "Let's bury the rat!"

Lucy ran across the length of the room, clicking her toenails on the maple floor. Net hunkered down and scooted under the bed to retrieve the old shoe box with the dead rat in it.

Lucy backed out from under the bed then soon headed for the door while barking, "*Ah, ruff! Ah, ruff! Ah, ruff!*"

"Shut up! Mr. Moloch will tie you up out back and you know it!"

Elisha Pearl told Lucy who stopped barking and gave her a brokenhearted stare.

Not until Paula helped me out of bed did, I realize I had on dirty clothes. I looked down and began to cry before falling to the floor where I started to rock and moan. I knew my folks, Great Aunt Annabelle, Kitty Momma, and everything else I'd ever loved were gone forever.

"Help her to get a-hold of herself," one of them told Paula, who nodded.

The next thing I knew, we were in the bathroom washing my face. Paula stood over me smiling like a shining star. She dried my hands with an old brown towel. She rubbed Vaseline Petroleum Jelly on my lips and told me it would soothe the nerves in them. What she didn't know was that I had very little feeling in my body anyway. She dabbed some myrrh gum on a sponge and rubbed it on my limbs to ease the limb pain and to help ease the swelling in my bones. She splashed apple cider vinegar mixed with rose water on my face to cheer me up. I figured she must know what she was doing, or she wouldn't be doing it. Besides, having her nearby to give me a little pat every once in a while, did seem a little comforting in a big sort of way. She looked old in her quilt-like dress.

Paula reached up over the commode and got a little tin. She opened it and took out a little piece of a fig cake and two clusters of raisins. She beckoned me to come closer. She fed it to me, telling me to eat to get some strength back from the fruit.

I obeyed her voice.

"Better?" she asked.

When I nodded, she bent low and whispered in my right ear, "'*May God which dwelleth in the City of Heaven, prosper your journey. And the Angel of God keep you company from here on out.*'"

I frowned.

She continued on with, "That's part of a scripture from the Apocrypha Tobit number 5:16. Raphael will go with you and keep you safe. The roads to where you are going are not dangerous. Crowded, yes. But dangerous, no. Calm down, stop your crying, Mary Myra Boone!"

I listened while nodding.

She looked straight though me and asked, "Understand?"

I nodded.

Paula rose, locking her eyes straight on me. "God's plan for your life can be summed up in one word: *Listen*. Understand?"

Again, I nodded.

She said, "The Alabaster box has been broken. You will walk in grace and light. Nothing will harm you. You do not look from your right or to your left... Look straight ahead into tomorrow. You have *a calling* on your life. When it's time to answer your calling, you, and only you, will know it. No one will have to tell you."

I listened.

"Your life's purpose is different from your calling. Your purpose is *why* you are here. Both go hand in hand. Mind you, the journey you are about to begin will not be easy, but God is with you. God has always been with you. God brought you here. I want you to remember this: The Alabaster box *has been* broken. Yesterday has passed. Today is here. Understand? It won't be easy to *listen*, but you can do it. You must do it! Understand?"

I nodded for the third time.

Paula smiled and motioned for me to look at a little silver oval-shaped locket she pulled out from behind her neckline. She opened it. "See my maw?"

I felt heat flush my face.

With a yearning voice, she said, "I just *know* my maw loved me. Even though she never came back for me," she told me.

When I looked at the oval locket, I cried.

"Don't cry. Do you hear me?" She dabbed at my tears with the hem of her dress.

I blinked.

"But I do know the *why of it* though. It was on account of this man she took up with from Huntsville, Alabama. And love."

I frowned.

She went on with, "*Beau*. Yes, Beau was his name. He used to tell her, 'I love you, but. ' Then he'd look straight at me and shake all ten of his skinny fingers like a Warlock casting a spell or something."

She gave an aspirated sigh, put her right little finger in her mouth, bit part of her fingernail off, and sighed again before spitting out the nail.

I listened.

"I'm not ever going to love anyone myself. What's the use?"

I nodded, understanding what she meant while biting at my bottom lip.

Paula mused, "Beau said a stork left me in a fir tree." She gave me an anxious look and asked, "Do I look like her or not? I *just know* I do. What do you think?"

I nodded and confirmed her hopes of favoring her maw. She flashed me a smile as wide as a rolling river, snapped the oval locket shut and said, "Thank you, kindly."

After hearing Paula's story, I remembered what I'd printed on my bonafide Prayer Ticket at the Salem Camp Meeting back in October: L-i-f-e. And I knew right then and there, in the Opportunity House, that even though I thought I'd failed everyone I'd ever loved in every way, I sensed that my own life, as empty and meaningless as it ever was, had begun again. There was a flicker of hope that somehow, I hadn't failed myself, and that I would be saved from the Opportunity House.

BLUE ROSES

Chapter 8

WE HEADED OUTSIDE where the others were standing beside a hole Elisha Pearl bent down and placed the old shoe box in the ground.

"*Ah, ruff!*" Lucy barked and ran back to the Opportunity House.

Faith held a piece of paper in her hands and began to read aloud: "'Ashes to ashes, dust to dust. If the women don't get you, the whiskey bottle must! Signed, your'n Poppadaddy.'"

"What in the world?" Susie bent down and with her hands pushed dirt on top of the old shoe box.

"Run and get a flower," Net told Paula.

"I will not pick one of my flowers for a dead rat!" Paula told Net.

"Never mind," Susie said, breaking up pieces of wood and then arranging them in the shape of a cross.

"Myra, would you like to see *my* flower bed?" Paula asked me.

Glad to hear someone say my middle name, I nodded and blinked.

"Just hold your horses! We got to say grace first," Faith cried out.

Net said, "Well, get to it then!"

I thought of Great Aunt Annabelle and felt a dark cloud come over me when Faith prayed, "Lord God all the mighty who made this here world we are a part of, please smile down on us today, including this here dead creation of Yours if You don't mind. And *pretty please* make for us a way to escape out of this here hell hole as quick as You can. Otherwise, we going to have to be asking Your forgiveness to come next week on Christmas day. We thank You, kindly. And everyone says, Amen!"

"Amen," everyone said but me.

"I've got to pee," Elisha Pearl whispered to Net.

"Go on then," Net whispered back.

Elisha Pearl ran off towards the house.

"Come, look at my flower bed," Paula said.

We headed towards one side of the house where she'd planted one row of flowers. The flowers were mixed in color. There couldn't have been more than half a dozen, if that many, rising out of the dirt.

"These came in the mail. I got to keep them," she told me, admiring her flowerbed before picking me a blue rose for my hair. It was growing next to a bright yellow flower.

I nodded.

"Between you and me, I say prayers over my blue roses. I figure if I can ever be as beautiful as a blue rose, then I'll make it out of this here hell hole. Mrs. Moloch says I got a green thumb. I'm not sure if I know what that means though." She looked at her thumbs and shrugged.

Susie offered, "I betcha it means you can grow things better than her like blue roses and purple and yellow violets."

"I don't know how that could be. All I do is dig a hole and plant the seeds then water them like the almanac says to do," she said.

Mrs. Moloch's voice came from an open window scolding, "Yaw'll best git on back up to the house and git your dinner started up."

"Coming!" Faith yelled back.

"Let's go," Susie said, waving towards the house at Elisha Pearl.

"We got chores to do, and if you like, you can help us," Paula told me.

I blinked.

"She ain't going to be much use with them hands of hers. She might as well be a retard!" Net blurted out.

"Stupid fool!" Faith shot back.

"I ain't a stupid fool!" Net argued.

"I'll beat the pure devil out of you!" Faith threatened.

"*Remember, listen,*" Paula whispered to me.

I nodded.

"Both of you shut your mouths before Mr. Moloch hears you and we *all* get a switch lashing," Susie told everyone.

I looked down at my hands and started to cry, not because of how bad they hurt me, but because I was coming to realize I'd never spell with Daddy, Momma, or Great Aunt Annabelle, let alone see them ever again.

ONCE INSIDE THE KITCHEN, I sat down at a wooden table to watch everyone cook us up a dinner. Looking around the kitchen, I saw cloth sacks of flour along with tins of rice and grain. Off to the side, there was a metal cabinet ajar that was packed full of tea, coffee, pots, pans and the like. There was a slab of bacon hanging from the ceiling as well. I saw another tin full of unshelled pecans next to a butter churn that had National Biscuit Company written in navy on it. The sink was as clean as a whistle with a big bar of Colgate's Octagon soap off to its side. Beside the soap sat a giant package of Uneeda Biscuits. I saw a clear jar of honey next to a green tin of pistachio nuts and a red can of almonds. There was a small yellow bottle marked, *Garden Myrrh for Chewing Only* and a sack of lamb's wool sat near a blue bottle marked, *Sweet Almond Oil.*

"Girly Girl, would you care for some chamomile, dandelion, sweet marjoram, or rose hips tea with honey?" Elisha Pearl asked me.

Paula smiled and gave a wave over my way.

I blinked.

Paula ran off into another part of the house and brought me back a book to read. She said it was an almanac and as best she could figure out, it had a lot of stuff from the Good Book in it as well as sunrises, sunsets, and, of course, moon risings. She stuck a pencil between my teeth to use to turn the pages.

I don't want to write with my mouth!

Not wanting to hurt Paula's feelings because she'd made me believe she cared about me, it was with a great effort that I turned the pages of the almanac with the pencil stuck between my teeth like one of the Moloch's had predicted.

Paula stretched her neck over and read, "*An Almanac for the Year of Our Lord 1639.*" Sighing while confessing, "This helps me a lot."

"She pours herself over that almanac every night that passes," Elisha Pearl said.

"And what do you do every night, smarty britches?" Paula asked her.

Elisha Pearl stuck out her tongue.

"I'll tell you *what* she does. She stands on a chair primping like a cheap, two-bit street corner New Orleans whore in front of the mirror in the bathroom!" Paula cried out.

Elisha Pearl flung Paula a hateful look.

"Turn the other cheek," Net interjected with a smile.

"Pray tell, who is going to peel these potatoes?" Faith said, holding up a pot of Irish potatoes with one hand and a butcher knife with the other.

"I will," Paula said, reaching for the goods.

"We are having beef tripe, mashed potatoes, Little Miss Sunbeam White Bread, and iced tea. Do you like beef tripe? We got Heinz tomato ketchup. Out of habit, we near drown everything we eat around here in it. Old habits are hard to break," Faith told me.

I shrugged.

Faith went on to say, "In case you don't know, Heinz tomato

ketchup is a lux-u-ry."

I nodded.

"You'll like my beef tripe. Why, I can fry it up good and crispy! Poppadaddy and me used to run Maw out of the house every time we fried up tripe," Faith said fondly then offered, "Or, would you like some fresh rabbit meat?"

I shook my head no and blinked twice.

"Girly Girl, are you sure you wouldn't care for some camellia leaves from our garden? We got plenty of pears growing too," Elisha Pearl said.

I shook my head no.

"Lord, I plum forgot about them pears! Will you run outside and pick us about a dozen or so? We can cook them up on the stove top with a little sugar and cream," Faith told Elisha Pearl.

"And cinnamon!" Elisha Pearl cried out.

"Go on and pick me some pears. Take Susie with you," Faith told her.

Elisha Pearl and Susie soon headed out the back door with a big, brown paper sack. "It's right nice to have company for a change. I do wish it was under happier conditions," Faith told me.

I started to cry and rock again.

Paula put down her butcher knife and ran over to me and began to pat me on the back until I hushed. She helped me blow my nose with a hanky with the initials *P. S.* embroidered in red on it before she went back to peel her potatoes.

"Do you like goat cheese?" Net asked me.

"How many times have I told you that goat cheese is for breakfast?" Faith blurted out in a scolding voice.

Net gave her a defeated look.

Paula peeled the potatoes with great care. She smiled at me when she caught my eye. I managed to muster a smile back at her while I listened.

"I believe I'll make a right good wife one day," Faith talked on while cutting up stringy meat that looked like someone's arm. She cut it in little squares and dipped one piece at a time into an egg mixture before the flour. She put it on a big plate and salted and peppered it before she fried it up nice and brown.

Elisha Pearl and Susie came running in the back door with the pears.

"I am believing if there is a God then my cooking will get me out of this place one day," Faith said wishfully to the stove top.

"Food is our friend," Elisha Pearl stated and patted Net's fat belly.

"I suppose so. But what I really want to do is have me a railroad diner so I can ride and ride and ride, never once having to look back at my life. Yes, with every mile of track the train rolls over, I could know I was on my way to a better place than here. I hate my life!" Faith confessed.

I blinked, understanding what she meant.

The others turned and looked at Faith when she smiled and said, "I'd call my railroad diner *The Moon*. I'd fill it with soul food and colorful lights like the stars above. Maybe let my customers name a light for a penny."

I managed another smile.

And even though we were children, after a while, with everyone working together, we were able to sit down to a table full of soul food that somehow, we'd managed to make all by ourselves. I suspected much of it would be drowned in Heinz tomato ketchup because old habits are hard for anyone to break inside or outside of the Opportunity House.

THE CHILDREN OF LIGHT

Chapter 9

SMILING THEN CLAPPING HER HANDS, Faith told us, "Like I've said before, it sure feels good to have some company. Poppadaddy used to say, 'Good company looks and feels better than a vanilla sundae!'"

I nodded.

"That's a stupid thing to say, let alone feel," Elisha Pearl said to her mashed potatoes.

"How do you know how anyone feels unless you look out of their eyes?" Paula asked.

Elisha Pearl shrugged her shoulders and made a little *tch* sound under her breath before stabbing at her potatoes with her fork.

"I'm hoping Santa Claus brings me a one-way ticket out of here. I want to be a doula if I can't get me a railroad diner like Faith," Paula announced.

"Oh, Lord!" Faith shouted, crossing her eyes.

Everyone looked at Paula.

"We got more necessities than *niceties*," Net said.

"But we get by," Elisha Pearl added.

"I agree," Paula said then bent over, and took a sniff from the blue rose she'd put in my hair. When she took my fork, stabbed a piece of beef tripe, and offered it to me, my eyes welled up with tears.

Mrs. Moloch stuck her head in the door to check on us while mumbling about stinking up the kitchen with soul food.

Faith stuck her tongue out after she shut the door.

The others giggled.

"*She* thinks *she's* perfect, but *he* doesn't," Faith whispered.

"*Do unto others as you would have them do unto you*," Paula read aloud from the open almanac next to my plate.

"I am doing unto her as she has done unto me! That mean old lady is lucky I haven't taken a butcher knife to her hefty chicken neck," Faith shouted out, slamming her fist on the table.

"What do you want to talk like that in front of our company for?"

Paula asked, turning a page.

"Don't preach to me from a weather book. Understand?" Faith warned her.

"I'm not. God does make the weather. Neither you nor I can top that," Paula said.

I smiled.

Net winced and gave us both a furious frown when Paula read on from the almanac, "*Faith is a Bible name*."

"Ain't," Net interjected.

Faith cut Paula a sharp look, but she didn't speak.

Paula, reading on, "It is too! Says so right here: *We live not by sight but by faith*."

"*We who?*" Susie asked Net.

"We, the children of light," Paula said matter-of-fact.

"All I know is my people came from Goshen," Faith put in.

Net frowned.

Paula cried out, "Besides, a person has got to have a promise to use faith. It says so right here."

Again, I smiled, knowing who she reminded me of—Great Aunt Annabelle.

"Geez! You all are a sight!" Faith said, rolling her eyes before saying to Paula, "And, you are the most superstitious person in the world is who you are!"

Paula gave Faith a tight smile before closing the almanac.

"Let's go carry Lucy these table scraps," Susie suggested.

"Mr. Moloch went out and tied her up while we were picking our pears," Elisha Pearl stated, wiping the table off with a wet rag.

"No wonder we haven't heard any barking," Net said, scratching her head.

"I hate for him to tie Lucy up like he does. It's just not natural," Paula said, running for the back door.

"You worry too much," Elisha Pearl told her. She opened the door for Susie who was carrying a heaping pot of table scraps.

"If I don't worry about us, tell me, who will?" Paula asked.

Who is going to worry about me? Who will pray for me?

Elisha Pearl rolled her eyes up at the ceiling.

"Wait," Susie said, and she ran back into the kitchen. She set her pot of scraps on the table, ran over to the icebox, took out some sweet cream and poured a dab over the scraps.

"Wait for what?" Net asked.

"Dee-zert," she whispered.

Elisha Pearl cried out, "Hurry it on up! My arms are gettin' tired."

"Hold your horses," Susie told her.

We all marched like toy soldiers on out of the Opportunity House into the backyard where all the trees were leafless except for an old stump with a shoot that held only one leaf.

When Paula saw me looking around, she walked over to the old stump and thumped once at the green leaves, causing it to dangle before informing me, "This is a Jesse Tree; it's about two thousand years old. Blue roses grow best beside it."

I blinked.

Paula went on with, "I pruned it myself," she said, stroking the old stump.

"Lord, you and your flowering!" Elisha Pearl cried out.

Paula walked ahead while calling, "Luu-cy, Luu-cy! Come here, Baby, and see what we brought for you. LuLu, LuLu. *Auauauuuhahaha!*"

Susie dropped her pot of scraps.

"What in the world?" Faith asked before she herself screamed.

The others gasped.

When I looked over to Paula, I saw Lucy hanging off the side of a set of cement block steps with a rope around her neck. Paula ran over and jerked the rope from the wiener dog's neck. But it was too late because Lucy fell to the ground as limp as a wet dishrag.

"Come here and help me!" Paula cried out in a desperate voice.

"Oh, no! Not our Lucy!" Elisha Pearl wailed towards the sky.

"Maybe if we give her some cold water," Net suggested while she paced.

Faith was pleating at her lips and crying as she stood over Lucy.

Paula was patting Lucy's head.

Lucy was not moving.

I vomited up my dinner.

"She's as cold as ice," Paula announced.

"Is she dead or not?" Susie shrilled.

Nobody said a word.

Paula stood up and sobbed into her hands and walked over to her flower bed without speaking.

"Ain't we better be going and getting Mr. or Mrs. Moloch?" Susie asked.

"What for? He's the devil who did this to her with that rope!" Paula shouted.

Faith considered before she said, "*He is, isn't he?*"

"I hate him!" Susie spit out and ran away.

"Go after her before we all get a beating," Faith told Elisha Pearl who obeyed.

"Get me the shovel," Paula told Faith, between clinched teeth.

Faith asked her, "What are we going to bury our beloved Lucy in?"

I wish I had some ice water.

Paula considered Faith's question before crossing her hands underneath her arm pits and ripping her colorful dress from her body. Stripped down to her slip and blue beads, Paula took her own dress, walked over, and wrapped it around the lifeless wiener dog's body. She said, "Lucy was my first real friend. She understood me!"

Elisha Pearl and Susie came back to join us.

"Oh, Lucy, I wanted you to get your freedom like I want for all of us, but not this way," Paula mumbled.

"Why did this happen?" Faith asked me like I knew and as if I would answer.

Pointing at me, Elisha Pearl asked them, "Do you suppose *she's* taboo? Reckon she fell off a gypsy wagon on its way to New Orleans?"

Net gave me a mean look.

Elisha Pearl gave me the evil eye.

"Hush! It isn't Mary Myra Boone's fault, so don't blame it on her. Can't you see she's upset too? It's that mean Mr. Moloch's fault!"

Paula cried out.

"And the Relief man's fault for trusting him with our pennies," Net mumbled.

Elisha Pearl raised her hands to the sky and said, "We need to get some strychnine to take care of Mr. Moloch once and for all. The hell with waiting for next week for Christmas dinner to do it!"

"He's a rattlesnake! I'm going to make him pay," Faith threatened.

Bless her heart!

I feared what might happen if one of them turned on me like a wildcat. Then, for the first time since I had awakened in the Opportunity House, I found myself thinking how nice it would be to go to the city of Goodlife. How nice two words sounded to my ears—her people.

Maybe I could look for a friend or two. Maybe I could even start school.

Paula walked over to her flower bed and got down on her knees and began to dig in the dirt with her hands. After digging a while, she got up and walked over and picked up Lucy who was wrapped in her beautiful colorful dress and placed her inside the hole. She covered the dead dog with dirt, while we watched aqua, gray, white, lilac, and yellow colored scraps of material disappear.

Mrs. Moloch's voice called out, "Marrr-y? Youngins get Mary cleaned up. Some of her people are driving up for her now!"

My stomach tightened while my heart raced.

Paula gave me a glance and nodded matter-of-fact at my hands before she said, "Life's journey is never easy for any of God's creations be it mankind or the animals. Four more words are all I have left to offer you: God is with you. Tell yourself: *God is with me* until you are dead and in the ground like our beloved Lucy. Stand tall, listen, and *never forget me.* Please Mary Myra Boone, *never forget me.*

Understand?"

I nodded.

The children of light obliged Mrs. Moloch and brought me inside. Once inside, they stood me in the front of an oval mirror. All I was able to do for myself was stand while my hair was being brushed, my dress smoothed out, and myrrh gum applied to my arms. I feltlike I had nothing in the world left to live for. There was a loud knock at the door.

Paula smiled at me and said, "Remember my words. Now go on with your journey."

God is with me.

"Gosh, wouldn't it be nice to have some people to come and get you?" Susie mused.

"Now that would be a miracle," Faith said.

Considering the thought, "It could very well happen one day," Elisha Pearl said.

"My almanac says, 'All things are possible with God,'" Paula said and patted me.

"Then, why are we still living in this hell hole?" Susie asked.

"I don't know," Paula replied.

"I still miss someone I loved in Goshen," Faith mused.

Even though I saw the darkness swimming back over me and leaving my muscles feeling like hundreds of rubber bands, I managed a smile as Paula slipped a handful of the garden myrrh seeds into my pocket and whispered, "*Shushushshush for chewing when you feel afraid.*"

An old, cracked voice called out, "Myra, child, where are you?"

Mrs. Moloch asked, "Who in the *hell* is Myra?"

Faith walked me to the front of the Opportunity House. The others followed. We entered a sitting parlor. There was an old man and woman both bent with age waiting for me. The woman looked like my Great Aunt Annabelle only older. Her eyes were like cracked rubies. Both the visitors were linen white. The old woman opened her arms to me like a morning glory and said, "Child, come here and give your Grandma Reatha a big hug."

Sensing a familiar spirit about her, I blinked and obliged her request.

"Bless her heart. She doesn't even know what to do, do she? Myra?" the old woman observed of me.

"Her hands are ruined for life," Mr. Moloch told them.

My body felt as stiff as a board. I didn't know what to think when the old lady said, "We'll get her to a good doctor as quick as we can. We'll even drive to Jackson if the need be."

"Ain't said a single word since she woke up. Suspect she's in shock," Mrs. Moloch said.

The girls nodded.

"Bless her heart," the gray-headed man said before adding, "Stricken with grief."

"I think she's a mute," Mr. Moloch stated.

Both old people exchanged glances.

Forgetting I had vomited up my food near the Jesse tree, "We fed her," Faith told them.

"Still, didn't make her feel talky though," Net said.

"Give her some peppermint water," the woman suggested to Mrs.

Moloch.

Someone asked, “Peppermint water?”

“To calm her nerves,” the old woman said.

Everyone turned to look at me.

Paula nodded, then smiled.

I locked eyes with Paula instead of blinking like I’d been doing since we’d met. I felt our hearts become one. I knew I’d never forget her.

Mrs. Moloch nodded while Mr. Moloch said, “I got a call late last night from the clinic over in Goshen. Me and the Missus went out and brung her over here. Cost me a pretty penny in gasoline beings we on a fixed income ourselves. Then, some dumb-talking Colored woman named Opal called before daylight this morning and said you all were her next of kin.”

The old woman who came for me gave him a sharp look before she turned back to me and said, “Myra, I thank the good Lord they found you alive.”

I observed the aged man who had come for me never took his eyes off the woman who talked so kind to me. When she spoke, he nodded his head in agreement with her every word. I saw the love he had in his heart for her.

He looks like the two-thousand-year-old Jesse Tree out in the back yard. And he's looking at her like Momma looked at Daddy when they told me their story of love and about Ray Charles under the pecan trees in the cool of the day before the fire.

The aged man caught my eye and gave me a kind, gentle look before saying, "Mary Myra Davis. I mean *Boone*. I am your Granddaddy Spurgeon Davis. This here is your Grandma Reatha. And even if you don't know who we are, you belong to us now. We prayed all the way over here from Goodlife to find the words to tell you. I know of no other words to say to you, but true ones. When it came to your folks and even with Annabelle, we made more mistakes than we care to remember. But we are begging you to forgive us for not loving you sooner, for not making things right and true, for failing our Marigold, and for not accepting her marriage to Virgil." His words left my ears stinging. His legs shook. His knees wobbled, and he fell to the floor.

I gasped. Fear filled my entire body and I thought that somehow, I'd killed one of my people.

The girls gasped too.

When he managed to stand again, he inquired, "Marigold, our beloved Mary, Virgil, and Annabelle were burned up in a fire. Myra, we were hoping you could tell us what happened. Can you remember?"

Grandma Reatha held her breath while he waited for an answer.

A new music entered my mind. A tempest. The music played amid screaming sounds of jeweled voices speaking in a deep, dark tunnel twinkling with stars, bright and definite. The images took me back in time only to blind my memory with flashes of green lights that rose from deep within my soul. The light was like the three clouds I'd seen rise and float out of sight amid the blazing red orange flames—flames I believed in my heart I'd caused when I used our gas heater for a play mailbox and mailed my letter and poem for Joseph Lester, the baby with the big head, and Smarty the sad dog into its vents.

Again, he asked me, "Myra, can you remember?"

Still, I was lost for words.

Then, he asked, "Can you tell your Grandma Reatha and me what happened?"

I shook my head no.

"One day?" he asked, standing to his feet.

No answer came.

The girls didn't move a hair.

My Grandma Reatha asked me, "Do you know how the fire started? Was it the Ku Klux Klan?"

The girls let out a long gasp.

I looked straight ahead.

Everyone waited for my answer.

The Molochs exchanged glances.

I began to blink twice for no.

Granddaddy Spurgeon spoke to me, "Child, no need to fret. What's done is done. Together, we are going to figure it all out. You are not in any trouble. You are safe with us now."

I nodded and closed my eyes, feeling afraid they'd soon come to hate me for not answering and for what I'd done or both.

My fear left me when he said, "Mary Myra Boone, we came here to take you back to the city of Goodlife to love."

Again, the girls gasped.

"Believe me," he went on.

Nodding, Grandma Reatha spoke these words to me, "In case our Marigold didn't tell you this: She is from Goodlife. Mississippi legend holds that the city of Goodlife is fifteen hundred miles square and fifteen hundred miles north, south, east, and west. Goodlife has a center. Neither you, nor do we, have to live inside, let alone visit it, yet. You will live with us at Magnolia Sunday and go to Needles School."

When he said the word school, I almost fainted.

A voice inside of me said: *Go*.

I nodded to my people that I understood. When we were heading towards a 1956 white-over-gold Bel Air Chevrolet Impala Sport Coupe, I wanted to ask the children of light to go with me, but all I was able to do was to walk away from them and the Opportunity House. I never even looked back, except to glance at Paula nor could I muster up the strength to turn and whisper, "I'm so sorry to leave you here."

I, too, was surprised that not even one of the girls said goodbye, not even Paula who I noticed had changed into a peach-colored dress of blossoming dogwoods. I felt dizzy. I closed my eyes. When I opened them, all I saw of the children of light were five little ovals of cool, bright, rainbow colors holding hands and singing and dancing in a complete circle while their song slipped on by mc like the slow sound of a clock ticking down, down, down into the dust of the earth.

Once inside Granddaddy Spurgeon's Impala, I turned and looked off to the side of the Opportunity House where I saw a small field of trees growing. I caught sight of one bright redbird resting in silence on the limb of a pear tree. Like birds do when they get a chill, the redbird was holding its breath and dozing. Since redbirds are made for wishing, I made one—that I could fly.

When the Impala started up, my Granddaddy Spurgeon and Grandma Reatha turned and smiled at me.

God is with me.

Granddaddy Spurgeon asked, “Ready, girls?” When he spoke, the sound of his voice was so kind that it made me warm inside. The redbird woke up and flew in front of the Impala.

When I crossed my legs, my dress stirred and whispered above my knees. I lowered my head, eyeing my wrapped, numb hands that had very little, if any, feeling in them. After taking in a breath of air, I rolled my neck in *my people’s* direction while jabbing at my bottom lip with my eyeteeth. I sat straight and strong in the car seat.

Grandma Reatha asked, “Ready?”

I blinked once.

When we turned, faced forward, and headed south out of Goshen to the city of Goodlife, I felt a like a redbird flying on the wind.

THE FUNERAL

Chapter 10

Winter-Spring, 1961-1962

WALKING INTO THE SANCTUARY of the Union Community Church, still without the use of my voice and hands, the first thing that caught my eye was the sun illuminating an oval window of broken purple glass. I watched the sunlight infuse its gold amid the purple's brokenness until soft sparkles of yellow broke into vein-like colorful streams leaving the church window glowing from a brown to a gray rose. I saw a spider weaving its web over a palm leaf and an olive branch engraving that was hugging a set of stairs that led off to a dark corner.

"Those are catacombs for the dead," Granddaddy Davis told me.

Grief-stricken and heartbroken, I nodded, seeing the underground passageways that lead to the catacombs that held the remains of somebody's loved ones.

My eyes locked on an altar where beautiful lifelike carvings of Godly images rested in an eternal sleep. Saint Paul was holding a book and a sword. Jesus Christ was handing Saint Peter a set of keys. Off to the side, I saw Jesus as a boy among the elders in the Temple, Jesus as a young man being judged before Pontius Pilate, and Jesus as an adult being hoisted to a tomb.

Like the stories Momma used to read to me from the Bible.

I recognized everyone at the altar. When I saw the sun through the stained-glass window lighting the Old and New Testament characters, I groaned when like a swollen river, memories of my folks flooded my mind.

"Myra, how are you doing?" Grandma Reatha asked.

I blinked and began to cry. Strange as it sounds, I wanted to bite someone like a mad dog. And even though my hands had commenced to heal some from the medicine and bed rest the doctors in Jackson had ordered, I was as filled with as much fear as the moment I had opened my eyes and saw the children of light staring at me in the Opportunity House. Then, I remembered Paula who had helped me the most. Even though I didn't understand all she meant, I felt a measure of comfort when I thought about what she'd told me was the one thing I should do: *Listen.* Listening wasn't hard for me to do beings I'd not said a word since the fire. I turned and set my eyes back onto the spider that was moving out of the sunlight to the darkest corner of the staircase to keep the remembering pain from taking over my mind.

God is with me.

"Myra, if for one minute you don't think you can tell your folks goodbye, let us know. We'll take you back to Magnolia Sunday," Granddaddy Davis told me.

I nodded.

Grandma Reatha asked me, "Myra, do you remember about me telling you that your Uncle John Shows spent many a year putting in these windows? And about how he special ordered them all the way from New Orleans, Louisiana, and some from Mobile, Alabama?" She put an arm around me. "Are your hands paining

you?"

I nodded and dabbed my tears with the bandages, which were

sparse, holding on tight to the knowledge the doctor in Jackson had assured us they'd heal save for the scars I was told to prepare myself for. No promises were made, nor could they be made when it came to *when*, let alone *if*, I would ever be able to write again.

Living deep within my own silence, I had worried myself day and night how or if I could ever go into the first grade since I couldn't even hold a pencil. It sure didn't feel like God was with me in Goodlife. And so far, I hadn't heard Him say a single word to me either. All I'd heard were the voices of others. I was listening, and I was waiting even though I knew God was the only one Who knew it was me who had killed the only three people I'd ever loved in this world by writing a letter.

"Half of John Show's life was spent in and outside this church house. He isn't your uncle by blood kin. We took him in as a family member once he fell sick with the cancer," Granddaddy put in then added, "A widower."

"Yes, it was. George Wilkerson, our druggist, who told him all about Trinity University. I mean the Duke University Chapel where he studied for four years all about filling prescriptions. George's stories along with the pictures he brought back are what gave Uncle John the inspiration to create the Union Community Church's stained-glass storybook windows," Grandma told me.

"The most beautiful windows in Goodlife," Granddaddy commented.

"That's Esther, Hannah, Naomi, Ruth, Hagar, and Rebekah," Grandma whispered to me when she saw my interest in one ray of sunlight that was shining through a white glass windowpane onto six women.

"Child, we'd better be sitting on down now," Granddaddy coaxed.

We followed him to a brightly polished pew. It smelled of cherry oil.

"George Wilkerson even paid for Uncle John to carve ornamental lead and gold symbols from the Bible into all the doors," Grandma told me.

I blinked.

A man with a kind, gentle face walked out from the catacombs and stood beneath a cross of gold. The cross had three rings straight through its center that united the arteries that led to a near-pulsating heart.

Is that God's heart?

To my surprise, black and white strangers began filling the church pews.

"That's Brother Jim Roberts," Grandma said, nudging me.

I blinked.

Once the sanctuary was filled, a thickening silence took over. I felt a damp coolness floating in the air. I felt scared and alone even though I was amid a crowd while I watched four men roll in three green velvet-lined pine boxes that held the bones of the only three people in the entire world I had ever loved. I felt like my heart was going to burst and cover everyone at the funeral with blood—a blood that I didn't even know the color of.

Brother Jim Roberts turned back to look to make sure he was positioned straight beneath the gold cross and the three rings with its now pulsating heart. He cleared his throat once and said, "The King in Hamlet says: '*My words fly up, my thoughts remain below: Words without thoughts never to heaven go.*'"

"Amen," said a voice.

Someone said, "Mum-hum."

He read on from a red leather Bible: "*He shall come again to judge the quick as well as the dead.*"

"I know that's right!" a Colored man agreed.

A fat, almost purple, Colored woman put in the words, "Preach it, Brother Jimmy!"

Tears rolled out from the corner of my left eye. I felt comforted when I saw my friends Quitman, Opal and Eddy slip in and sit behind us. Between them, they were toting three cardboard boxes with windows cut out on each side. Opal began crying like a newborn baby.

I sobbed and kept thinking I was having a bad dream and at any given moment I'd wake up and be right back in Meridian with my folks and Great Aunt Annabelle shopping in town.

Breaking into my thoughts Opal bent forward and whispered, "Bay-doll, you gots to be st-rrrong for them."

I blinked, remembering Daddy called me Bay-doll because he couldn't speak clear like the rest of us. He couldn't call me Babydoll like Momma did. My remembering pain was great.

"Oh, dear God in heaven!" Grandma cried out to the ceiling. She began to sob on Granddaddy's shoulder while he patted her on the back. "Why?" she asked his shoulder, looking at me with those ever-piercing ruby cracked eyes of hers.

"There, there, there, Reatha," Granddaddy told her in a comforting voice.

"We are *all* are living in perilous times and none of us can escape the eye of the Lord God," Brother Jim Roberts went on. He picked up his Bible and kissed it before saying, "Folks, like it or not, we are all a part of an eternal existence. *We will* spend eternity in Heaven or Hell. Long ago, William Shakespeare knew it was so. He wrote about it for years. But today, I want to inspire you with the hope that the three souls that were once at the center of these three bags of bones are in heaven, together for eternity."

"God love them!" Grandma cried out and about scared me slam to death.

"The Bones, I'm told, were good people," he told the crowd.

Granddaddy cleared his throat and corrected him, "*Boones*."

"Ah, yes, the *Boones* were good people. And the Lord God, our *honorable* heavenly Father saw fit to go on and call them and Annabelle Reynolds Davis Stringer to heaven to be with Him in *Paradise*. That's all there is to it," he went on.

Half the crowd picked up their Bibles and drew them to their lips and proceeded to kiss their Bibles too. Not me though. Instead, I kept my eyes bent straight on the three-green velvet-lined pine boxes and wondered *why* total strangers had come to talk and cry over three people that they had never met once. It was at the funeral when I realized all I had left in the world were stories, good and bad, to call up to keep me company in Goodlife.

To my right sat a lion-like man with stark white hair sitting with a good-looking blonde boy and a young girl with ruby-red lips. I felt their eyes on me. When the man caught my eye, he lifted an arm and wrapped it around the girl.

"I hear tell she may be retarded. She's never even been to a school before either," I read from his lips.

The girl turned and smiled at him.

A sharp pain pierced my heart when I read from the girl's lips. "I heard her paw had some Colored blood in him."

Waving my way, "Folks, keeping with the heartbeat of the Union Community, we have to love and accept Miss Myra Boone. That's all there is to it," Brother Jim Roberts said.

I did not wave back. I wanted to die. I wanted to be a bag of bones too.

Someone whispered, "Myra Doom."

I heard yet another whisper of, "Cloaked in doom."

They don't even know me!

"And I mean it! Everyone from Soso to Goshen to Glossolalia as well as from where the 'People of The Way' reside has got to be kind and tenderhearted to this here Boone girl. This is one time that we got to work together and show her love. You all hear me?" Brother Jim asked the crowded church.

The heart behind him pulsated on as if it was filling with human blood.

"We do," some of them cried out while shaking their heads.

Someone asked, "Can we love *her*?"

A Colored man clapped his hands together in midair and shouted, "We will!"

I don't want them to love me!

"My-ha Ba-boon," someone whispered.

No one could ever know the deep sadness I felt in my heart at the funeral.

Amid the backdrop of the ever-pulsating heart, Brother Jim said, "This funeral gathering is the most beautiful sight that I have ever seen with all of us—the Lord God's children gathered together in one sanctuary. This is how it was meant to be. I am sorry yet happy that it took death to bring us to life here today."

Someone cried out, "You got that right!"

"We all know that all of us in one place may never happen again in Soso. But for the funeral to lay three good people to rest, some of us knew them and some of us didn't, and, and, and for this here young girl—Myra Boone—we would not be here today! I think we should give the Lord God *thanks* for these three folks dying," Brother Jim talked on.

Someone cried out, "Thank you Jesus for the fire!"

"Saints of God, we *must* forget the tales that have been told to us. We *must* do the best we can now that her heavenly Father has sent Miss Myra Boone to Goodlife to live at Magnolia Sunday among the rest of us until her time comes to cross over to the other side into Glory to enter Heaven's center."

Suddenly, I saw a black cloud appear above our heads.

Once again, Grandma began her sobbing. Even though it was so bad, she was able to cry out, "Marigold, Poppa and I got Myra with us now!"

Then, a hard, furious shaking took over my Granddaddy Davis. The shaking was so bad that I knew he was going to fall out and hit the floor. No one did anything to stop his shaking either. I closed my eyes, held my breath, pierced my bottom lip with my eye teeth, and prayed for a friend to help me along my way. Still, I didn't speak.

"Marigold, we so sorry! We so sorry! We so very, very, VERY sorry!" Grandma cried out.

"Sweet Jesus of Nazareth hold her broken heart," someone said.

When the hard shaking turned my Granddaddy loose, he let out a groan then cried out, "My sorrow is incurable! Dear God in heaven have mercy on me for failing my Marigold!"

Behind me, I could hear Opal sobbing like a newborn baby with Eddy now sharing her tears. His boots were tapping the church floor like a rattlesnake's rattle. I could smell the sweat beading across his black forehead.

Wiping his eyes and looking like he was about to fall on out on the floor any second, Granddaddy let out a second groan, "Ooooooooh me, ooooooooh my! Why did she have to die? My only one. Why, why, why?"

I heard Opal sobbing while rocking her pew. "The Lord God knows. He do know the truth about it all, but He waits. Yes, He do. His patience is eternal and everlasting."

I'm in trouble now!

Pointing to the pulsating heart, Brother Jim Roberts told us, "Folks, life is uncertain, death is sure, eternity is forever, and Heaven and Hell are a heartbeat away. Our big brother, Jesus Christ said, '*Be thou faithful unto death and I will give you a sacred Crown of Life.*'"

That must be Jesus' sacred heart!

Everyone shouted, "Amen!"

The black cloud lifted itself from above our heads.

"My baby girl, Margie Anne, asked me before I come up here today if I thought we'd know each other in heaven," Brother Jim told us.

"Oh, yeah! Oh, yeah! Oh, yeah!"

"Folks, I'll tell you straight like I told my Margie Anne. The Bible says that, '*We will know as we are known*,'" he went on.

"The Bible does! It does say it. The Bible does say that!"

Someone asked, "What does that mean, you think?"

It was Brother Jim who answered, saying, "I believe it will be like it was on the Mount of Transfiguration. Saints of God, do you remember reading when Moses, who had been gone 1500 years from Earth, came walking down the Mount of Transfiguration? And Peter, James, and even John did not even have to be introduced to him. No sir, folks! At once, *the Bible boys* recognized him as Moses. This alone tells us Moses had not lost so much as his name, let alone his identity! His friends knew it was him!"

From the crowd came shouts of, "Hallelujah!"

"Saints of God, let's fill this here sad day with *the hope of gladness* when Myra Boone takes her walk down the street of gold, Straight Street, in the City of Heaven that she will know her family as she knew them in Meridian. What a glorious day to look forward to! Myra

Boone will live her life to die!" he cried out.

Everyone agreed with an, "Amen!"

What in the world is he talking about?

"Now I want to end with one request of each one of you: Don't allow the bond of affection...What I mean is, don't let the *hope* that comes with Jesus Christ be broken any more than the Enemy has tried to break it by leaving this young girl an orphan all but in the crib of life waking up with only the angels in Goshen to tend to her," Brother Jim Roberts went on before he told me, "Myra Boone, look around you, these are your *neighbors* in Goodlife."

Some whispered, "They wuz all burned slam up but her."

"Hoo-boy! You don't say?" a voice cried out.

I felt my low back muscles tighten against the polished cherry church pew when I heard the words, "Is she going to change her last name to Davis now?"

Someone announced, "The doctor in Jackson told them her larynx may have been damaged by the smoke."

"You don't mean it!" said a voice.

Someone pointed out, "See them white rags here and there on her hands? I bet when they take them off, her hands are going to be a sight to see!"

I wish I was a bag of bones inside one of them pine boxes!

Brother Jim Roberts gave the command, "Everyone, please stand to your feet."

"Courage. Today you need courage, Bay-doll," Opal whispered to me.

Heading in the direction of Granddaddy's Impala, I turned around and gave Opal a tight smile.

"Sweet Jesus, she ain't going to say another word ever again!" Opal wailed out to the sky.

My pain is too great for words.

Eddy said while sobbing and kneeling down beside me, "Miss Myra, we wuddin' able to find Kitty Momma. She must have run off, but if she ah comes back, Opal and me will brang her to you."

I nodded.

It was Opal who said, "But we did find three of her newborns alive but orphaned." She and Eddy pointed to three cardboard boxes.

I managed a smile.

The lion-like man walked over and stopped him by saying, "*Boy*, what do you mean addressing an orphan girl without her grandfolks' permission?"

I burst into tears when Eddy rose, straightened his six-foot form, and backed off from me before drawing his right arm back to strike at him, but Opal stopped the blow.

"You two Coloreds ain't from 'round here, are yah?" the lion-like man asked them.

No answer.

I gave Opal a furious frown. She shook her head no at me.

"I ain't ever seen either one of you with Brother Jalla Moses or his bunch from The Way," he went on.

Granddaddy Davis walked up and joined us with, "How you are doing, Cecil?"

"Very well," Cecil replied, tipping his hat.

"Are you meeting our granddaughter, Myra, and her Colored friends?" Granddaddy went on.

"Why shore I am," he lied, smiling at us.

"Good. Glad to see you trying to be kind," Granddaddy told him.

"Brother Spurgeon, I shore do appreciate a fine a man as you are speaking good about me," Cecil said.

Granddaddy smiled and said, "Folks, this here's Mister Cecil Davis, but we aren't kin folks. We share the same last name as a lot of folk do in this here part of the South."

Cecil Davis nodded at the lot of us and said, "How do?"

Stay clear of him, a voice said to my heart.

Opal blurted out, "Mister Davis, tell us now. Is pride the same thang as dignity?" She turned and set a hard look on Cecil Davis.

Eddy ginned like a spider monkey.

"Tch, tch, tch," were the only sounds that came out of Cecil Davis' mouth until a muffled steam of words ran out together which sounded like, "Damndisgracetothehumanrace is what I call *them.* Damn disgrace. Part of the curse," he said before resigning himself to a group of white men.

"Cold-hearted fool," Eddy said.

Grandma joined us.

I managed a smile, not at the people who had showed up for the funeral, but at Eddy who was still my daddy's best friend other than Ray Charles who I knew I'd never get to meet anyways unless the Lord God saw fit.

Once inside the Impala, we headed to the Union Cemetery. When the car turned onto a gravel road, I heard all shapes and sizes of rocks crying out beneath the wheels and being thrown along the wayside. The second we arrived at three freshly dug holes of orange clay with the three pine boxes nearby, Grandma Reatha went into a fit of sneezing.

"Is there a cat around here?" she asked Granddaddy who shrugged.

Kitty Momma's litter of three!

After we were seated in chairs with the red word *Soso* painted on their backs beside a complete circle of colorful roses, I turned and gave the cemetery the once-over. Out of the corner of my left eye, I saw a shadow near a little shed beside the Piney Woods where a gray wolf was roaming around the shed's front door. I was surprised when the wolf rolled its neck around on its shoulders then yawned when a little girl with thick Coke bottle-like glasses cut the corner and entered the shed. She was carrying a blue coffee tin.

"Myra," Grandma began then said, "I know you don't know *why* we are all doing this or even if you know *why* we are gathered here in this graveyard."

I nodded.

She paused to lock her empty ruby red eyes on me. "We are here to say our goodbyes to Marigold, Virgil, and Annabelle," she told me, sobbing beneath her words.

Wiping her eyes with her sleeve, she went on with, "We've had three of our Colored hired hands, Shebuel, Hiram, and Lucas to go and get a statue of Jesus Christ from Jackson to watch over their graves from here on out. Jesus is holding a Bible in His hands. Does that set well with you?"

Still, I had no words to let go of.

While we three walked towards the pine boxes, I memorized the seven etched words on the single headstone that bore my folk's names: *Pompa mortis magis terret, quam mors ipsa.* Many years later I learned their meaning: It is the accompaniments of death that are frightful rather than death itself.

The people in attendance were as silent as the sleeping souls in the Union Cemetery. I wanted to break their silence and speak, but I couldn't seem to let myself win the battle of words that I was caught up in.

Besides, what to say?

To my surprise, I felt a tug at the hem of my dress. I turned and saw the girl with the thick Coke bottle-like glasses. Over her head, I could see the statue of Jesus Christ being lifted by three Colored men from a truck. And like Grandma had said, Jesus was holding a Bible. It was open.

I blinked, wondering if the gray wolf was nearby.

The girl offered me her right hand to shake and said, "Hello, my name is Margie Anne Roberts. I'm the preacher's baby girl. Sorry if I'm late. I was feeding Mozella and other neighbors who live in and around the cemetery. Would you like for me to show you around until you get well enough to register at Needles School?"

I nodded, reaching for her smooth, perfect-looking hand with my bandaged right hand.

I was surprised when Margie Anne Roberts sighed and took hold of my right wrist. And it was in the Soso cemetery amid a complete circle of roses that Margie Anne reached out to me and became my first *and only* friend since I'd entered the city of Goodlife.

The biggest surprise of all came when I looked up and saw Opal and Eddy passing out the three boxes with their cut out windows that held Kitty Momma's orphaned kittens to Shebuel, Hiram, and Lucas the Colored hired hands of Granddaddy who soon placed the statue of Jesus Christ holding an open Bible in His hands on my folks' grave for all the world to see.

I knew the chance of me having a kitten to take back to Magnolia Sunday was slim to none because Grandma Reatha was allergic to cats. Even from a short distance, she had told me right off that cats made her sneeze for hours. I felt a measure of joy enter my heart knowing Kitty Momma's three orphaned kittens had now found a good home like me. And for that reason alone, I knew God was with me even if I never said another word to anyone.

THE HOUSE OF JOY AND LIFE

Chapter 11

FEELING LIKE A BLADE of tender grass, I walked into the front parlor of the Honorable Judge Larry Falkner's house where Lavender, Patsy, Elizabeth, Sissy, June, Billy, Edward, and Will Falkner stood amid a bunch of folks ready to sing. They all were gathered around a black and white striped baby grand piano, all looking like a herd of nervous sheep.

"Sssshshshshshsh," some of them muttered.

"Act ordinary. They are here," came a whisper.

Everyone turned and smiled at me.

Clunk, clunk, clunk came from Judge Falkner's mallet when he hit the top of the striped baby grand three times before saying, "All-right-ie folks, let's give a happy song."

Grandma Reatha turned and gave me a blank look while Granddaddy Spurgeon shuffled his feet, unable to sit down because there were no chairs in the parlor.

"Wheee-w," Granddaddy blew into the herd.

But they did not sing. Instead, every single one of them began whistling the tune *Down in My Heart* while Judge Falkner accompanied them on the baby grand with the intensity of Jerry Lee Lewis.

"Child, everyone is trying the best they know how to take our minds off our pain," Grandma Reatha said with a serious sweetness in her voice.

A beautiful little red-headed girl backed out from the herd, turned, and walked over to us and curtseyed before she said, "Hello, my name is December Rose. Please, be welcomed to the House of Joy and Life."

"Oh, my goodness," Granddaddy Spurgeon said. She bent her knees once more.

I looked up and saw a beautiful red-ceiling window filled with gold and silver lines that branched into a Roman wheel. The open window glowed like a red rosebud. When, without warning, the window's wavy curves and intricate patterns began to open and turned to me. I sniffed.

The music and whistling stopped.

"My bow-pocket dungarees have mother-of-pearl buttons sewn in pairs," December Rose told us.

"Did your maw make them?" Grandma asked her.

"No," she replied.

"Who then?"

"Mail-ordered straight out of New York City!"

"Oh, my goodness," Granddaddy put in when she smiled and turned in a circle for us to admire her bow-pocket dungarees.

She looks like she could float out of here.

I managed a smile.

"I will feel as carefree as a sparrow on any Easter morning before sunrise with my dungarees. Besides, you don't have to wear a slip with them," she said, prancing out of view.

Her red hair looks like a burning bush.

The herd of folks headed to the back of the House of Joy and Life where I heard pots and pans amid a clanking of glasses, plates, and silverware.

Grandma bent down and said, "Myra, try and oblige Lavender and the rest because like I told you, this is all they know how to do to ease our pain."

I nodded.

December Rose pranced back into the parlor and said, "Follow me."

Entering the Falkner's dining room, I saw a glorious table filled with main dishes, vegetables, breads, desserts, and fruits. Off to the side were two little cherrywood tables. One table was filled with coffee, iced tea, Frostie Root Beer, glasses of goat milk, and a silver pitcher of ice water; while the other table held breads, rolls, cheeses, saltines, sugar-coated fat green grapes and purple sugar plums. There was a chocolate pecan pie with a maple-brown colored crust that somebody had cut one thin slice from. In the center of the main table was a Virginia ham studded with cloves and pineapple. Alongside of a pink pork loin roast, sat a platter of golden-brown fried catfish, a big pot of chicken and dumplings, Southern fried chicken, and a heaping stack of barbecue spareribs. And there were pots and pots filled with the likes of yellow squash dotted with baby pearl onions, speckled, purple butterbeans, white rice with brown gravy, whole sweet potatoes, and French-fried potatoes.

"We decided to make an early Christmas dinner since it's right on us," an old lady confessed to Grandma, picking a pecan from the top of a pie. She drew it to her nose and sniffed then put it into her mouth, smiling and nibbling.

"Christmas is Myra's birthday," Granddaddy said.

I closed my eyes and prayed to disappear so I wouldn't have to celebrate an early birthday dinner in pain.

"Do tell!" the old lady shouted then mused, "We should do something extra special for her then. I have some scissors and paper in my purse."

Nodding, Grandma asked, "Where's the turkey?"

An old lady cried out, "My Lord have mercy! We plum forgot the turkey!"

Grandma gave us a blank look.

Granddaddy shook his head no at her.

I saw Margie Anne Roberts standing beside the desert table squinting her eyes while reaching for a purple sugarplum. I saw Christmas cookies in the shape of Southern pine trees and fat fudge brownies graced with pieces of fresh, bright red cherries cut in the shapes of quarter and full moons. There were lace cookies that looked like thin pieces of golden-brown street pavement on a copper serving tray with a cut-up chocolate pie that had ruby red whole strawberries dotting its center. I saw star cookies, gingerbread man cookies, sugar-coated shortbread, and saltwater taffy surrounded by ribbon candy that smelled of clove.

I want me one of those fat brownies with a quarter-moon cherry.

"If you all will, gather round so I can say the blessing before it gets any later," Judge Falkner told us. Once we obliged him, he prayed, "Dear kind, heavenly Father, please help Myra Boone feel loved by her neighbors from here on out. And everyone says, amen!"

The crowded bleated, "Amen!"

When I opened my eyes, I saw an ugly man walking towards us. His nose was pointing like a cockroach from a stout head. His skin was dry and hollow and tanned. Long legs stuck out from his flat body. He looked as though if he hit his knees to pray, they would transform into wings. A half a dozen gray and black hairs were combed over towards the left side of his head that only held a few teeth.

Grandma left the room.

It was Granddaddy who introduced us. "Myra, this is Enoch. Mister Enoch Vine."

When I acknowledged him with a nod, I felt a divine presence.

"How do you do?" he asked and gave me a jack-o'-lantern smile that made me want to laugh. He observed, "You look like a Babydoll, 'cept for them bandages on your hands that make you look like you're an Egyptian mummy ready to step into a Memphis boxing rang with Sugar Ray Robinson!"

Granddaddy offered, "We all are as well as could be expected, wishing everything was all right, but it isn't. Myra almost lost the use of both her hands in the fire. The tips of her fingers you see sticking out are about all she's able to use right now. The doctors in Jackson said her body will heal itself though. She will be fine enough in time. We aim to keep her with us to heal before sending her out into the world, let alone to school. We're not for sure if the smoke did any damage to her larynx or not. She's remained silent. We don't aim to force anything, let alone words, on her. We are glad to have her in Goodlife with us to love."

Without giving my hands a second look, Mister Vine clicked his tongue once on the roof of his mouth and asked, "Where's the Shepherd's pie?"

We ain't got any Shepherd's pie here, Stupid Enoch Vine!" an old lady blared out at him.

Frowning, "Then, I ain't interested in eaten' nary a thang you got," he told her.

"Stupid Enoch, suit your ugly self then," she told him.

Again, frowning, "Got any chicken and rice?" he asked, sliding his eyes at me.

"Nope."

"Venison soup? Chili?"

"Stupid Enoch Vine, you are an iron horse, is what you are!" she told him.

"What kind of a Christmas-birthday-dinner is this?" he asked with an all but toothless smile and took one plate off the top of a stack of pretty blue plates that were beside a little rosemary Christmas tree. He bent down and sniffed at the rosemary Christmas tree and came back to us with a suspicious look before he reached and broke off a little piece of rosemary, brought it to his nose, and took a deep whiff then said, "Whooo-ff! Smells like mint jelly to me. Now if that don't beat all!" It was with great care that he placed the broken piece of rosemary in his front shirt pocket like a souvenir.

Does he know Christmas is my birthday?

"Stupid Enoch, git your'n hands off Lavender's rosemary Christmas tree for Christ's sake!" another old woman cried out.

Mister Vine ignored her and gave a little snort.

I blinked twice, smiled, and wondered how, or if, he was talking about my birthday.

He caught my eye and asked, "Babydoll, what would you like to eat?"

Unafraid in his divine presence, I told him without a second thought, "Shepherd's pie just the same as you."

And like a tornado he whirled around and said, "You ain't gonna get it here, but if you ever get over to Goshen, *Sketches' Place* serves up the best Shepherd's pie in the South."

"Myyy-ra, where are you?" Grandma called out.

"She be in here," Mister Vine offered, handing me his plate.

I tried to take it with the tips of my fingers but couldn't.

Pulling the plate back from me, he asked, "You ever walked through the darkness?"

I considered his words before I gave him a so-so head shake.

"I am walking through the darkness right now. As is my brother Sergeant Festus Vine, who lives in Antioch, but since he ain't here to defend himself, I won't tell you anymore about his problems with love, money, and the whiskey bottle. If there's one thing I ain't, it's a tail bearer. You know, a gossip. But if you like, I can tell you about mine as soon as we fix us up a plate. Listen, we can head on outdoors to the red picnic table away from the others."

Silence.

I watched him dot one tablespoon of everything onto his dinner plate, making it look like a child's finger painting dotted with samples of colors amid a blue painter's wheel. "I'll fix you a plate myself before I tell you all about it," Mister Vine informed me with a tooth piercing his bottom lip which was chapped and bleeding. He held up a breezy blue-clear plate for me to admire.

Grandma walked into the room as he said, "Follow me. We can sit and talk a spell. You hear?"

I bit my bottom lip with my eye teeth and rolled it almost inside my mouth but not without wondering what he could tell me about the darkness.

"Or if you ain't in the mood for it, I got plenty of other old-world stories that might suit your fancy. Are you interested or not?" he went on with Grandma listening and smiling before grabbing two Frostie Root Beers for us.

I nodded.

Grinning, he asked, "Would you like to hear about the darkness or not?"

"I'm thirsty. Can I have a cool drink of water first?" I asked.

Gasping, Grandma screamed out, "Myra, you spoke! How does your throat

feel?"

Mister Vine set his eyes straight on me.

"Sore."

Mister Vine was smiling at the nice and neat, dotted dinner plates he'd created for us. He headed on towards a little side door and as he kicked it open, he called back to me, "See you at the red picnic table. Remember, the red one."

I nodded.

Pouring me a nice glass of cool water, Grandma cried out, "Thank the good Lord, you can talk!" When she put it to my mouth, I drank every drop.

Smiling while giving me a tight hug, she whispered, "Myra, listen to me, you go on outside with Mister Vine and enjoy his company. He is a good man. He wouldn't hurt a flea, let alone kill a fly." There was a break in her voice. She mused when another old lady joined us then said, "Mister Vine is ugly; that's all he is. Some folks say he's the ugliest man alive. I've never known Enoch to hurt so much as a bumblebee though."

"Ah," I said, eyeing the pot filled with baby, purple butterbeans.

"And he *loves* to talk," Grandma told me.

"Stupid Enoch does have a pure heart that faith needs to work miracles though. He got a revelation by way of a mistake to believe the

Lord God for anything down in New Orleans on a Mississippi steamboat years ago," an old lady offered before walking away.

Granddaddy joined us.

Grandma encouraged me, saying, "Go on outside, find Mister Vine. Enjoy the dinner he's prepared for you on the pretty blue plate."

"I will try," I said.

Stunned Granddaddy cried out and grabbed at his heart. "That child's voice sounds like our Marigold's did at her age! Oh, my goodness, she spoke!"

Nodding at Granddaddy, "Myra, go on outside and listen to one of Mister Vine's stories. We've all heard them more times than we want to remember," Grandma told me adding to Granddaddy, "Spurgeon, leave her be. She's going home with us. We can talk to her then. Let Enoch spend some time with her."

I waited to see if either was going to ask me any questions about the house fire.

"Myra, listen to your Grandma Reatha," Granddaddy Spurgeon told me and led me outside the House of Joy and Life where the sun was shining brightly to join Mister Vine who was saving me a seat at the red picnic table.

TENDER GRASS

Chapter 12

LEADING ME OUTSIDE the House of Joy and Life, Granddaddy Spurgeon was smiling for the first time since I'd laid eyes on him in Goshen. After I sat down on a bench in front of Mister Vine, he made sure our Frostie Root Beer drinks were uncapped before walking away. I set my eyes straight on Mister Vine, anxious to hear about the darkness, and waited.

Whispering while leaning forward, Mister Vine said, "Babydoll, glad you came. I wish I could tell you everything was all right in my soul, but one year ago my old lady run off and left me alone in the darkness."

I shuddered at the close sight of a face that made me want to scream.

Sensitive to the look I gave him, he said, "If you don't want to look at me, I'll understand. It will be nothing new to me. I know how I look. I may be ugly, but not without feelings. Funny thang, most folks figure ba-cause a body is ugly that he doesn't know it. Listen Babydoll, I *know* I'm ugly!"

At once, his words entered then sat down upon the table of my heart. "Mister Vine, would you please tell me about your walk through the darkness?" Tears welled up in my eyes. Strangely enough, I felt comfortable and safe with the ugliest man alive.

"Be happy to. Know what my *one and only*, Baleen, said to me?"

I shrugged and said, "No."

Without caring how I looked to anyone, I dipped my face into my plate of food and ate like a hog ate slop. I ate like I'd been forced to do since the fire.

"I'll tell you what Baleen said to me. She said, 'Stupid Enoch Vine, you are a dreamer. A good-for-nothing, damn dreamer is what you are! Your face is worse than the horseshit in the pasture. I can't bear to look at it anymore!' Can you believe my *one and only* said *that*?" he asked me, then slammed his fist on the red picnic table.

Feeling flushed, I shook my head. "Once, my momma told me,

'Everybody must dream or die.'"

"You damn straight! Destiny is nothing more than a dream fulfilled."

As I watched him closely, his ugliness faded away.

"Baleen was always leaving me alone, not to mention the fact that she even blamed me for the Second World War!" he cried out.

"Why?" I asked, chewing.

"She said, 'The voice of God tells me things.' What could I say to *that*?" he told me, taking a tablespoon of an unidentifiable vegetable.

Frowning, I asked him, "What God?"

"Dogged if I know! Why, the way she cursed, *her god* must have been Satan!"

"Ah, ha," I said thoughtfully.

Mr. Vine continued. "I said, 'Baleen, are you trying to wear my brain out, or what? My patience is running thin, now.'"

Mister Vine frowned when I took another face dip into my plate, so I said, "Don't mind me. Go on. I'm listening."

He said, "Yep. That's what I said to her. I have asked the Lord God many a time, "*Why?* What have I done to deserve this kind of a life with this Old Testament wife who was born a member of that crazy Church of the Only Ones who tries me at times to the tip-top of my bent?" Mister Vine stopped speaking, then mused, "I knowed what Ole' Jonah must have felt like in the whale's belly!"

"What did the Lord God say?"

"Nothing."

"Ah, ha."

"Why, FDR never even sent me no letter to ask me if I even wanted to sign up for the Second World War. Not that I can recall of, anyway. How was I supposed to go and defend my country if I had no idea that it needed my help?"

I nodded.

Mister Vine shrugged his shoulders and offered opened palms to the sky before whispering, "*She*, Baleen, that is, had a *high school diploma!*"

I lowered my face to my plate and took a bite of my thick, Southern cornbread and proposed him a half smile, hoping Mister Vine would not find out I'd never darkened the doors of a schoolhouse in my entire life. I was right thankful that he didn't seem too easily offended by the way I was eating.

"Know what I believe?"

"What?"

"I believe Baleen had a curse on her."

I choked on the cornbread while remembering that preacher man at the Salem Camp Meeting saying I was cursed by my folks or such. Still, I was unclear what he meant by shaming me.

"*Why else* would she treat me in such a way?" he asked, pausing before concluding, "*Unless* the doctor dropped her on her head at birth!"

I shrugged.

Together, we looked over to the House of Joy and Life and could see the people gathered in little grape-like groups watching us talk from the windows while eating from their breezy blue see-through pretty dinner plates with the proper eating utensils.

Mister Vine helped himself to a heaping tablespoon of chocolate pecan pie then said, "Many a time I thought and thought about it all, mulled it over and over in my head, but I never got one lick of peace until she disappeared one week before last Christmas on a Wednesday, December 18, to be exact."

"*December 18?*" I asked, realizing the date sounded familiar to me.

"Yep, right a'fore we were aiming to put up a short-limbed Loblolly tree with crystal clear lights that glowed like diamonds in the dark."

My eyes widened.

"Left me not one but two notes, one typed and one printed. Both written on white linen fancy store-bought writing paper. Baleen knowed I could read some," he told me.

"Me too," I said, wondering how I'd take a sip of the Frostie Root Beer. "In Meridian, I used to copy entire books from the Bible myself," I told him proudly.

"*Really?*"

"Really."

"Why would anyone want to do *that*?"

"There was nothing else for me to do. Besides that, Momma wanted me to learn how to write. Mister Vine, you might as well know, I've never been to school yet."

Nodding, he said, "Me either."

I smiled and felt grateful for his honesty.

"Anyhow, Baleen wrote me a *Ba-cause* letter saying, 'You get married *ba-cause* you don't want to be alone. You get married *ba-cause* you can't have a family by yourself. You get married *ba-cause* you want someone to sit with you at church. I must have been drunk on new wine when I married you *ba-cause* when I woke up in the same bed with you, all I remember is I wanted to vomit when I realized what I must have done on that Mississippi steamboat with my eyes closed flat of my back in the darkness of a hot as hell Saturday night all liquored up!"

Memories flooded my mind.

"Never mentioned one word about love nor trust nor character, let alone dignity." He paused before saying, "She wrote in the printed letter, 'Stupid Enoch, I can't be married to the ugliest man alive. I must leave the Glass House. I wanted children. Can we have any? NO! Why? *Ba-cause* you look like a cockroach! I may have been dumb enough to let you get me drunk enough to marry you, but I am not stupid enough to put an innocent child through the ugliness that comes naturally with the Vine family.'"

I listened on.

"Baleen was the most physical gal I've ever seen, always smelling like mint jelly and rosemary!" Enoch slammed a balled up fist twice on the picnic table, causing both our plates to rattle before he told me, "Besides, the steamboat drinking and gambling was *her* Saturday night hot-to-trot idea, not mine! I remember Baleen saying while pointing a shaking a bewitching finger at me, 'I want *you* for my husband!'"

"Glass House?" I asked, cutting my eyes to the people in the windows who had their faces pressed close to the windowpanes. From where I was sitting on the outside of the house, they looked fuzzy, blurred, and unidentifiable to me.

"Yeah, I built the Glass House myself. Baleen and I only slept together once," he mumbled adding, "on the Mississippi steamboat where I feared I'd wake up in the icy and dark waters of Nineveh!"

I smiled, but he didn't notice. He didn't seem to care one bit what he said to a young girl like me. Or even if I understood.

His tone of voice changed to a biting, bloody sound. "Baleen threatened me with, 'Stupid Enoch Vine, husband of mine, if you don't give me a divorce, I swear before God that I'll smash your head through the most precious window of that Glass House of yours so even your own maw won't recognize you! Or how would you like to wake up in the bottom of the ocean in a hundred of more pieces like a jigsaw puzzle of the French Quarter in New Orleans inside a wooden box?' Why, Baleen's tongue could walk the earth if her mouth was set against the sky!"

I gasped.

His bottom lip cracked and became dotted with blood when he let out an exasperated sigh to the sky and gritted what teeth he had left together. He looked like he would collapse any minute.

"A ruby is what Baleen ain't. Dipped her hand in Bonnie Parker's blood after her and Clyde's demise in 1934," he muttered. Then, hanging his head low where his chin pressed into his chest, he added, "Baleen's strength was firm with her pride chained to her bones like a blanket. Listen, if I didn't know better, I'd swear on a stack of Bibles that she was Satan's daughter!"

"Mister Vine, I'm sorry for your pain," I told him, now seeing it eating away at his flesh.

"Oh, never you mind me none," he went on, lifting his head up and reaching for his Frostie Root Beer. "After all, you've already been through losing your entire family like you did. Besides, pain and suffering is what makes us whole."

"I am sorry for your pain though."

"Besides, I'm partly to blame for making a mess of my own life," he confessed.

I interrupted softly with, "I know how you feel."

He cut my words off. "My maw, Tap Lee, put a bullet straight through her own temple, mind you, right before Sergeant Festus' and my very own eyes. She had spoiled me so doggone bad, maybe because she couldn't remember who my daddy was, that when I got older, I didn't think I had to brush my own teeth like everybody else. See what happened?" Mister Vine showed me his all but toothless grin.

After shaking my head to erase his toothless smile, I frowned.

He went on to tell me, "I blame Maw for giving me 'Stupid' as a first name too. How could anyone do that to her own flesh and blood? She marked my destiny at birth even if it was my daddy's name!"

"When it comes to blame, I do know how you feel," I said, showing him my bandages.

"Do you believe in angels?"

"I might."

"I do," he told me, bracing the back of his neck with both hands united by his fingers. He began to rock forward then backward on the picnic bench while sucking his teeth clean. "Sergeant Festus says, 'Angels are sent from the City of Light, Heaven, to purify our bodies through everything that is of good report and no s-e-x is involved."

Closing his eyes tight and continuing to rock on while saying, "And to teach us that love calls us to the things, good and evil, of this world." He stopped speaking and thought a minute before he went on. "Satan's angels from the City of Darkness, Hell, are a stone's throw away ready, willing, and able to steal everything good the Lord God wants us to have if we ain't careful. Sometimes, they come in the darkness like I was telling you about, but then other times they stand in the center of the sun's light and fool us with sweet talk and a pretty package. They want to take all that we have, including our very life! Like with my Baleen. She walked through the front door of my heart and took me straight to bed. Then, she hung me and my heart out to dry like a summer's washing!"

I closed my eyes, too, in hopes of seeing a face, any face of someone I still loved while I listened for a familiar voice, but I didn't see anything but the selfsame darkness that Mister Vine was going on about.

"After Baleen left me, the Lord God sent me my own angel who taught me how to finish up the Glass House. His name was Metatron. I'd begun building it before the first of the seven days. Would you like to see it?"

"I suppose."

"The door to the Glass House is always open."

"Mister Vine, what are you going to do now that you are all alone?"

"Without my one-night wife?"

I nodded.

"To tell you the truth, Baleen was nothing more than a rusty nail in my hands ever since day one. She wasn't my first mistake, and she won't be my last mistake either. But at least I know that she was a mistake," he told me, pulled out his handkerchief, and then blew his nose.

I listened on.

"After serving my earthly prison time of a few hours after I married Satan's daughter down in New Orleans on the Mississippi River, no less, I got a revelation about my own wasted life. I've made a lot of mistakes. I learned to *believe* by way of faith in the Lord God's power. I learn how to pray. I guess Baleen was worth the trouble she caused me." Mister Vine paused and took a long look at my bandages before he said, "Two lumps of clay that are always going to be in the center of the Potter's wheel."

I shrugged.

A faint smell of his root beer breath passed through my nose as if to bronze it when he said, "Myra Boone, I thank you kindly for listening to me. I thank you even more for calling me *Mister Vine.* Not many folks have ever treated me with respect like you did and straight off at that."

I nodded.

In a voice filled with pure compassion, he told me, "The Master doesn't want you dipping into your food like a hog. Watching you eat like a hog even gets on my nerves of steel!" He reached into his front pocket for a handkerchief. Then, with a great gentleness, the ugliest man alive wiped the food from my face.

Unafraid though embarrassed, I let him.

"Listen, the Master I serve can give you your hands back. Can you believe if I speak it so?"

My mind took me back to the Salem Camp Meeting. I looked around for some olive oil for anointing. I saw none. Thinking I was smart, I said, "We don't have any olive oil though."

Enoch shrugged, looked around, and took hold of the Frostie Root Beer bottle before he said, "We will have to make do and use the foolish things of this world to confound the wise. You want this unworthy, old, and ragged soul to believe then ask the Master to reach down and touch your hands with His healing power?"

Without any hesitation, I said, "Ask."

Mister Vine took the Frostie Root Beer bottle and touched a bit of its contents with his pointer finger. He dabbed a dot of it on each of my bandages. I closed my eyes and released my faith without a second thought when he asked, "In the name of the Lord God, wilt thou hands be made whole?"

I nodded, and in my mind, I released my faith to believe.

A great excitement entered my hands while a cool breeze whispered and stirred above our heads. When I opened my eyes, I saw a soft light engulfing my hands.

Mister Vine asked, "Well?"

I shrugged.

He waited.

"The pain is gone."

He smiled and began to unwrap the bandages.

I said, "Thank you kindly, Mister Vine."

"Thank the Master, not the vessel."

After a few minutes, all we saw of what the fire had done to my hands was ugly scarring.

With a knowing smile Mister Vine asked, "Anything else?"

"How about some Frostie Root Beer? I am right thirsty."

He reached for the root beer and handed it to me. I took it, drank, and for the first time in my life, I knew God was real.

Mister Vine said, "Know what my brother, Sergeant Festus Vine, told me about Baleen?"

"What?"

"He said, 'Enoch, Baleen's treatment of you is only a mirror of the agony in her own mind. Jud'st thank the Lord God for letting her leave like He did and count it up as the greatest Christmas present of your life! Her leaving is the pure grace of the Lord God working in your life. Let that two-bit demon whore go back into the darkness of Hell from whence she came!"

I gasped.

"Yes, love calls us to the things, good and evil, of this world. Indeed, love has everything to do with God's grace. Babydoll, why do you think you lost your family?" He stopped talking and locked his glassy dark eyes like two platinum keys hard into mine.

Silence.

I looked away, breaking the lock as a mantle of guilt set itself on my shoulders. "I killed my family because I mailed a letter, my *one and only* first letter and a poem verse, *The Clown*, in the vents of a gas heater without thinking months before the first frost fell. And I was, and still am, afraid to tell it."

"Well, looks like you made a mistake, and you got some big time explaining to do. At least you know that you made a mistake. That's like winning half the battle in your mind. I know because I've been fighting battles in my mind for years. If I were you, I'd ask the Master to show me what to do next," Mister Vine offered me.

I nodded, knowing I could trust him not to tell on me. I thought about Baleen being a rusty nail in his hands. I reached out and took one of his hands and turned it over, but I didn't see any scarring from a rusty nail in it. I figured the nail bearing Baleen's name must have been driven much deeper than the naked eye could see when unexpectedly I saw into the center of Mister Vine's heart. It was at that moment it became crystal clear to me the outside of a body had nothing to do with the inside of a body, and indeed, the ugliest man alive had a heart filling with light.

I turned Mister Vine's hand loose and bent over and plucked up a blade of tender grass. I offered it to him. He took the blade, sniffed it, and placed it inside his front shirt pocket with the broken piece of rosemary he'd taken earlier from Lavender Falkner's little rosemary Christmas tree. When I looked at his ugly face, I saw tears the colors of the rainbow streaming down his cheeks straight to his now-lighted heart.

Together, we stood. Mister Vine's hands dropped alongside his body. To me, it felt like time was standing still. And when I looked into the grass for an image of his shadow, my eyes stopped short of his head, which had an angelic sun-ring about it.

I felt like my folks were somehow near; I was moved to lie down in the tender grass. Mister Vine joined me, and together we looked into the sky and said nothing. We enjoyed the simple pleasure of being together watching the clouds float over us. Lying in the tender grass in the city of Goodlife, I felt peace in my soul. The earth moved. I knew I wasn't going to be lonely anymore. I felt as rich as cream.

After a short while, Mister Vine stood and helped me to my feet. Before he walked away, he cleared his throat and nodded once to signal me that I had to go meet the rest of my neighbors inside the House of Joy and Life. I never expected to see a miracle the day of the funeral outside the House of Joy and Life, let alone that no one inside the house would be the least bit surprised by it. All my grandfolks offered me in the way of an explanation were two sweet smiles.

My neighbors were glaring, almost cleaving, in their little grape-like groups from the windows blended with extra special no doubt faceless paper doll cutouts they had hung from those selfsame windows that spelled out, Happy Birthday, while they continued to clean their breezy blue glass plates of food with the proper eating utensils.

NEEDLES SCHOOL

Chapter 13

January 1962

AFTER MEETING my neighbors at the House of Joy and Life, I was filled with a good measure of faith to begin my first day of school at Needles. However, my grandfolks said I couldn't go visit a classroom until late May. I wasn't as lonely as I'd been in Meridian. There was always somebody to listen to. Southerners love to talk, and my neighbors were no different.

Still, a deep sadness filled me when I thought of how my folks had gone on into the City of Heaven without me. I knew it was my fault for mailing my first letter down the vents of the gas heater before the first frost before Daddy could clean it up for lighting. I hadn't spoke up and told him or Momma or Great Aunt Annabelle what I'd done.

No matter how I tried to put it out of my mind, it always came back. You can't forget some things. And worst of all, when you want to talk face-to-face to the ones you love instead of others like your neighbors no matter how lonely you are, once they disappear from your life, you can't. It was hard for me to understand *why* I was born if I was to always live in an ocean of loneliness.

Even though I'd never even been inside a schoolhouse, I believed going to school was going to be the answer to my loneliness and my remembering pain. Part of my remembering pain was remembering that on cool days Momma had parked the Ford across the street from a schoolhouse in Meridian and let me watch children play in the schoolyard. On some days I'd get to watch them get in a straight line and walk into a door. Then an hour or two later they'd walk back out the selfsame door in a straight line no less. I had no idea why they got in a straight line to walk in and out the selfsame door. That puzzled me. Oftentimes, I daydreamed of walking in and out of the selfsame door of a schoolhouse like I'd seen other children do while sitting in the parked Ford with Momma on a cool day.

Lying in bed at Magnolia Sunday, I imagined that a schoolhouse was a medicine cabinet and the books inside held words instead of Bayer aspirin and cherry cough syrup that would bring healing to me. I prayed that one day I'd hold a book of my own and read from it and that it's words would be the medicine I needed to feel better about myself.

I had hope that I would get the answers to all my questions I'd never been able to ask anyone in Needles School regardless of where the books were published or who had written them. I had rolled my first day of school over and over in my mind. Still, I was nervous I'd embarrass myself by saying or doing the wrong thing. I suppose that's why I decided to say very little, if anything, once I got there. I didn't think good thoughts about myself any more than my folks had thought about themselves. I felt like a *Nobody* that we endured in Meridian from the careless white whispers about my daddy. I felt like I had failed my folks in more ways than one when I didn't ask the Lord to heal Daddy's deafness and to make good on my part of Momma's deal with Him. And the ever-present mistake I'd made writing my first letter was always looming in my thoughts. Knowing Momma's secret dream was to move back to Goodlife to get away from our once shared daily bread of sadness, the realization it was me who was now living there didn't make me happy one bit. I didn't know how to forget what I remembered or even if I should forget.

Besides, how do you forget people you love?

May 1962

THE SUN WAS SHINING, and the birds were singing for my first day at Needles School. It didn't take me long to realize how Needles got its name.

My teacher, Lavender Falkner, was a gem. She said even though it was late in the school year, I could enroll anyway. She even let me begin with children my own age instead of the first-grade students. Looking back, I am not so sure that was the best place for me.

First-off, my purse was stolen from underneath my desk. Next, when I went to get myself a drink of cool water from a bubbler drinking fountain in the hall, someone snuck up behind me and pushed the back of my head into the water and left me wet from my neck to my waist. Recess turned out to be the worst part of my first day at school when four boys, each taking me by an arm or a leg, picked me up and flung me into a silver garbage can.

"Myra Boone cloaked in doom!" some boy shouted in the school yard.

"Cloaked in doom," came an echo.

"Retard, retard, retard!" some of them chanted.

"Still not talking, eh?" another voice asked.

I was surrounded by hot laughter and stinky garbage.

No wonder Momma left Goodlife for Meridian.

Someone tore into my heart with, "Who'd ever want to touch, let alone hold, those ugly *deformed* hands of a bab-oon girl?"

I felt hopeless. There was no one to save me. No one to even help me out of the silver garbage can. The certainty of faith I'd felt with Mister Vine after laying in the tender grass behind the House of Joy and Life seemed far, far away. I was even lonelier at Needles School than I had ever been in the Piney Woods of Meridian.

"Maybe *she* is a *he!*" someone shouted.

It was Margie Anne Roberts who first came to my defense with, "Leave her be!"

"Look over here, blind girl! Ask Jesus to make your four-eyes into two. *Lord God, make the blind girl whole!*" a boy cried out to Margie Anne.

"Did Jesus pass you by like a piece of garbage like He did the retarded bab-oon girl with the deformed hands?" the tall boy asked her.

"Did your maw wake up with a stranger on the other side of the railroad tracks instead of her preacher man again?" someone else teased her.

Charging them like a powerful bull and eyes filled with red rage while yelling with confidence, Margie Anne cried out, "I'm not afraid of you!" She fell on her face, but she was quick to roll over and face the rascals before they could kick her.

From the garbage can, I watched unable to utter a sound in my own defense while everyone continued to laugh and make fun of us.

This is my first day of school.

"I'm not afraid of you!" someone mimicked her.

"It's because she can't see! How can someone be afeared of what they can't see?" a voice asked.

Again, everyone laughed.

Someone shouted, "Maybe Myra Doom is the daughter of the ugly Stupid Enoch Vine and the long-gone whore Baleen!"

They roared with laughter.

These boys are as mean as rattlesnakes.

Looking over at me, Margie Anne said, "The story of my life. That's how they've *always* treated me."

A tall boy yelled, "Whoever heard of a twelve-year-old first grader!"

"Nobody! Nobody! Nobody!" they chanted.

Stinking like sour milk and food scraps from the silver garbage can, I didn't know what to do.

Margie Anne picked herself up off the ground and faced the crowd of children. When she opened her mouth to speak, a handsome boy with rosy cheeks charged then kicked her on her blind side. Her legs snapped out from under her. She hit the dirt.

Unable to defend myself, I felt hot tears on my face. I'd never been taught how to defend myself. I felt like a fool.

A small boy with navy blue cowboy boots appeared out of nowhere and came to Margie Anne's defense with, "Why you sons-ah-bitches, take your ugly smart asses out of here before I shoot the lot of you, then gouge your eyeballs out, put them in color-coated egg cartons, and send them by United States mail to fill up your maw's mailbox come next Easter! Go on! GIT ON OUTTA HERE, you sons-ah-bitches and ugly smart asses!"

Laughing while scattering with the crowd, one boy called back, "A short queer and a blind Christian! Two disciples right out of the Good Book, no doubt about it!"

The small boy yelled, "You sons-ah-bitches! You better look both ways 'afore you cross me and my friends!"

Margie Anne wiped at her cheeks while rubbing the trunk of her neck then said, "Myra Boone, meet a new friend, Johnny Paul Russell."

The small boy sighed like an infant angel when I said, "Hello, Johnny Paul Russell."

"Howdy do! I seen you at the red picnic table eating with Mister Vine. From behind the bushes, that is," Johnny Paul told me.

"I *saw* you," Margie Anne corrected his English.

Each took hold of one of my hands and helped me out of the silver garbage can. They helped me to my feet and steady myself.

"The bushes?" I asked.

"Yep. I weren't invited to the funeral, so I couldn't come to the early Christmas-Birthday dinner for you either, but I watched and listened from the bushes with my friend Raven," he replied.

"*Wasn't*," again Margie Ann corrected him.

I began fidgeting with my hands.

Johnny Paul gave Margie Anne a puzzled look when she said, "Johnny Paul, people don't *invite* people to funerals. Don't your daddy tell you anything?"

"*Doesn't*," he corrected her back.

She rolled her eyes at him.

"Nope, Paw only tells me sad stories about the mess he's made of his life."

"Well, they don't!" she shouted and began to clean the dirt from her bloody knees.

Johnny Paul commented, "Jesus Christ, what a bloody mess!"

He turned and looked at me and said, "Please to meet you, Myra Boone. I drank the rest of the Frostie Root Beer you left on the red picnic table. It wuz hot, but it still had a right smart twang to it. I sure enjoyed the bit of brownie and the pecan that you left on your plate after me and Raven joined our hands together and believed right along with Mister Vine and you for your healing. I, for one, was right glad he didn't use olive oil when he prayed for you because I was right thirsty for some root beer. Frostie is my favorite!"

When he offered me a handkerchief, I took it, wiped my eyes, then said, "Thank you, I guess?"

"Who is Raven?" Margie Anne asked him.

"Pleased I could be of a service to you—then and now. I'm always happy to believe in the impossible. Never seen too many possibilities at my house." He stopped speaking for a moment and shrugged. "Girly, Raven is a girl who lives along The Way. You two gots to meet her one day. She's everyone's' neighbor because she lives deep within the woods," he told us, trying to get an eyeshot of my hands. I held them out for him to see. When he saw them, he smiled while holding his nose.

With all the courage I could muster up, I said, "I didn't know school was going to be like this. I'm not going back. The children at Needles are mean!"

"I don't blame you one bit, Girly Girl! 'Quit while you ahead.' That's what Paw has always told me. And to stay shed of the other side of the railroad tracks where the whorehouses be!"

Giving us an understanding but not a look of support, Margie Anne asked, "How will you two ever learn, Mr. and Miss Smarty Britches, if you don't go to school?"

"I don't want to learn," Johnny Paul told her before turning to me to say, "Girly Girl, you stink like my paw! He always smells like two thangs, garbage and whiskey. Hey, you need a dip in Taylor Creek for sure."

"*Things*," Margie Anne corrected him.

Shrugging, I told them, "I'm sorry. I'll go back to Magnolia Sunday and get myself cleaned up as soon as I can. I'm sorry you two got hurt on account of me."

"Oh, this is a good day for us," she said, smiling at Johnny Paul who was nodding in total agreement.

"You got that right! Girly, remember when the sons-ah-bitches tried to pull their foolishness on me?" he asked Margie Anne.

Margie Anne pushed her thick glasses back up onto her nose. "I remember."

"What did you do?" I asked him.

"Went home to get Paw's shotgun, come back, shoved the barrel in between their flowery leader Cody Mack's eyes, and then said, 'As God in heaven is my earthly witness, I swear I'll blow your damn brains out if you say one more word about my paw, you red-faced, flowery, yellow-balled bastard! You can say goodbye to your life on this here earth right now. Say the word.'"

"What did he say?" I asked.

"Called my paw a drunk and me a queer. Cody Mack told everyone how Paw wrecked his truck in front of his house and spent the night in the ditch until Sheriff Delk hauled him off to jail to sober up. I don't care what name they pin on me, but they better keep their mouths off Paw. I love my paw! And I still don't know what a queer is."

"What did he say when you stuck the shotgun in his face?" I asked.

"Called me a cocksucker! Then, he ran off to hide behind the others he runs with. I don't remember flowery Cody Mack ever saying anything worth a hill of beans. Do you, Girly?" Johnny Paul asked Margie Anne.

"Not a word worth repeating," she answered.

"Mercy!" I said.

"Myra, Johnny Paul's daddy is Russell Russell. He is the janitor over at the Merchant and Farmer's Bank of Mississippi in Ellisville," she told me.

"What's a janitor?" I asked.

Johnny Paul gave Margie Anne a shocked look before saying, "Someone who serves folks for a little bit more than nothing. Someone who puts on a Sunday morning smile when folks slip him their spare change for his Saturday night fun." He stopped speaking and cracked his knuckles twice before he said with pride, "Paw oversees the garbage at the Merchant and Farmer's Bank of Mississippi in Ellisville."

"Oh, that sounds like an important job," I said.

"Damn right it is!" he cried out.

Margie Anne frogged his arm and said, "Stop with your cursing!"

Eyebrows lifted and looking serious while rubbing the arm Margie Anne frogged, Johnny Paul asked me, "Any more questions?"

"Why weren't there any Colored children in Needles?" I asked him.

Looking at Margie Anne, he said, "That's the way Soso is—can't or won't mix it up. 'Sides that, they want to stay alive. Ain't that right, Girly?" Johnny Paul answered me.

Nodding in agreement with Johnny Paul's answer to my question, Margie Anne asked me, "Myra, are your hands healed for sure?"

Showing them my hands, I said, "Yes, I think so. They still hurt me though especially at night. See how ugly they are?"

Johnny Paul eyed them for a long while before saying, "I betcha you ain't gonna be writing much with those. If I was you, I'd go on and quit school before I got hot good and damn started. Teach them a lesson or two! Face it, you *are* pretty old to be in the first grade. Even a dumbass like me knows that!"

"Johnny Paul!" Margie Anne yelled.

"Quit while you ahead," he repeated.

"Don't make a snap judgment," she told him.

"Girly Girl, you gots ta know I'm a-speaking the truth," Johnny Paul said.

"I need to wash my knees," Margie Anne said without correcting his English. She didn't correct him the first time he said *gots* either.

Walking away, Johnny Paul told us, "I got to check on Paw myself.

I'm sure Mister Everett Bass has done gone and sold him a fresh pint of corn whiskey. I suspect he ain't any more interested in studying being a bank janitor and garbage man today than I'm interested in studying William Shakespeare at Needles!"

Even though Johnny Paul Russell walked away from us without saying a proper goodbye, I felt good about him coming to my defense. I knew he'd walked away not because I smelled of garbage but to look after his paw. After my long-awaited first day of school at Needles, I knew right then and there that I never wanted to stand in a straight line going in and out of the selfsame door once, let alone twice a day. I was no longer puzzled by the straight line either because I knew for sure that any straight line at Needles School, or any school for that matter, was not for me.

SUNDAY, MAY 23, 1962

Chapter 14

IT WAS SUNDAY, the Lord's Day, and church-going time.

My eyes popped open long before our rooster, Freddy, sounded his usual early morning alarm to wake Magnolia Sunday. Looking beyond my pink carnation curtains at the early morning dew dotting the blue morning glories, I saw the sun shining on a fence post that once guarded a cotton field that now divided cantaloupe and watermelon fields. Since I grew up believing redbirds, the cardinals, were made for wishing, every time a pair flew into the blue glories, I made my wish that the Lord would give me encouragement that one day I could be a writer and help others feel better about themselves unlike me.

The Sunday morning smells of coffee, buttermilk biscuits filled with sweet, creamed butter and orange blossom honey, and a pineapple-raisin upside-down cake baking filled Magnolia Sunday.

I washed my face with lilac rose water. My best dress was lying on top of the deep freezer taking care of itself. Saturday night I'd pressed four Bible story books on top of it to capture the warmth of the freezer's motor. This was an ironing trick my momma had taught me. Most days, I felt guilty for even opening my eyes and breathing. I had always thought going to school like other children would be the answer to my prayers, but my first day at Needles opened my eyes to what the real world outside of myself was like. For once, I was glad that I was alone with myself and God, who as far as I knew, hadn't said a single word to me, yet.

"MYRA, WHERE IN THE WORLD ARE YOU? Has that child wandered off to Taylor Creek to get a little fishing in before church?" I heard Granddaddy Davis tease Grandma Reatha.

"Well, Spurgeon Davis, she'd better not have! And if she has, it's because *you* taught that *sin* to her," Grandma Reatha said.

I walked into the kitchen as she was pouring him a cup of coffee.

"Reatha, how many times have I told you it isn't a sin to fish?"

"I know fishing isn't a sin! Have you forgotten today is Sunday and the Lord's Day?"

Granddaddy gave me a wink and said, "Elvis Presley sings *and* fishes on Sunday."

I laughed.

When Granddaddy held up a magazine with Elvis Presley's picture on it wearing a white sailor's hat and smiling on a boat with his guitar in one hand and a fishing rod in the other, Grandma reached into the fruit bowl for an orange and threw it at his head.

"Good morning," I said.

"Myra, where have you been?" Grandma asked.

"Shaking out my dress like I do every Sunday morning," I said, cutting my eyes over towards Granddaddy when he caught the orange. He threw it into the air a couple of times and gave me a grin and sniffed at the sweet smell of baked pineapple in the Sunday morning May air that the box fan was filling the kitchen with.

"Myra, we have an iron. I wish you would use it instead of the deep freezer and those raggedy Bible storybooks. Why won't you use an iron?" she asked.

"I use what I *remember* how to use."

Granddaddy came to my rescue with, "Reatha, let the child be."

"Do you two monkeys think you can get the Impala ready while I take the pineapple-raisin upside-down cake out from the windowsill?"

"Yes, Ma'am," we declared in unison.

Granddaddy Spurgeon stood from the table and whistled my way before throwing me the orange. And together, we threw it back and forth until both of us disappeared deeper into Magnolia Sunday to do our best with what the Lord had blessed us with.

AT EIGHT O'CLOCK, we three piled into the Impala and headed to the Union Community Church in Soso. Granddaddy Davis said, "My, my, my! If you two aren't the prettiest girls I've ever set my eyes on!"

"*Girls?* Why Paul Spurgeon Davis, that is the nicest thing you've said all morning!"

"I still know a *pretty* girl when I see one," he added, winking over at me.

I smiled and asked, "Granddaddy, are we going to stop by Sister Ruby's house to give her and Johnny Paul Russell a ride?"

"We are."

Grandma nodded, and then smiled.

From the Impala, we watched Jack and Jill, Granddaddy's white-faced collies, barking and wagging their tails, hoping, no doubt, that if they showed off a little, we would change our minds and stay home from church with them.

Granddaddy promised from the car, "You two git on back up on the porch right now! Do you hear me? We'll be back after a while with you a Pepsi-Cola with ice cubes from Blue's Corner Store. Then, I'll take you to Taylor Creek for a swim."

And with their master's words, the white-faced collies turned to each other and barked. Jack made a complete circle turn, and Jill bowed to him before they both turned and ran to the front porch to wait for Granddaddy to make good on his promises.

"*My white jewels*," he whispered into the dashboard and hit the gas pedal.

In no time, we saw Sister Ruby Russell's house. Johnny Paul was standing in the middle of the road dressed as smart as a Shetland pony. He was wearing his best white shirt, Levi overalls, and navy blue cowboy boots. A red bandana was tied around his neck. He looked like he was going to the Mississippi State Fair instead of the Soso church house though.

Grandma had to say, "Look at Johnny Paul with his *ironed* white shirt."

When Granddaddy blew the horn, Sister Ruby made her way to the car. Johnny Paul ran close behind her. His boots were too big for him. They were bobbing on his legs as he ran.

"Good morning, neighbors," Sister Ruby beamed a sweet ruby-red lipstick smile beneath her purple Sunday 'Go to Meetin' Time' hat without showing any teeth whatsoever. It was months ago that old Doc Farmer had mailed them off to Mobile, Alabama, for a better fit. They got lost in the United States mail with only God knowing their whereabouts. I kept thinking some poor soul would get a box in the mail marked *Occupant,* think they had ordered a package from Alabama, and rush indoors to open it. A scream would be heard for miles when Sister Ruby's teeth smiled up at them with the unspoken pleasure that only she would appreciate. Nevertheless, we pretended not to notice that she had no teeth. That was our way of being polite.

Old Doc Farmer had developed a bad habit of forgetting to put the right name on his return address labels after he lost his wife and secretary, Pansy, last spring when she fell off their best mare, Felicia, on her way to their rented mailbox at the United States Post Office in Ellisville. She was run over by a watermelon truck on its way out of Soso, then, true of false, thought to be the Watermelon Capital of the

World. When old Doc Farmer found Pansy, his eyebrows raised and his facial muscles froze with shock and had yet to thaw out, leaving him looking scared to death and a sight to behold.

The Farmers had married young, thirteen and fifteen, and practically grew up together. The love they shared was as deep and as calm as the water of Biloxi Bay before hurricane season hit. However, old Doc Farmer's mission in life had since become to sow good seeds of faith by giving away all the money they'd saved for retirement to move to the East Coast to get away from the Mississippi heat, tornado and hurricane seasons and live in the snow. Anywhere East that had snow was to be their final home. Folks thought it strange that anyone from the South would move to the East to live with hopes of enjoying its harsh winters and snowfall. They had no children or grandchildren to share their golden years with, so he spent his days giving free medical care to the poor, mentally retarded, widows and orphans throughout the state. He told anyone who would listen that there was nothing short of dying from a rattlesnake bite worse than losing the one you love in pieces and busted up like a watermelon. He seemed happy enough to me, save for still looking scared to death and refusing to eat watermelon, let alone open the mail. His neighbors looked after him and his mail.

Once we arrived at the Union Community Church in Soso, I saw it was white all around with mid-May's daisies and honeysuckles growing below the pink crepe myrtle trees that our dying neighbor, Uncle John Shows, a self-made yardman, had planted years ago. The rest of the Union Community had all gathered enough money to buy some Louisiana mail-order purple, pink, and white wisteria vines. Uncle John had draped them around the building. It looked like a beautiful scene in *Gone with the Wind* before the American Civil War busted in on Atlanta. The most important project Uncle John had undertaken before he was struck down with the cancer, was installing stained glass Bible story windows from looking at a picture our druggist, George Wilkerson, had brought back from Duke University in North Carolina when he was studying how to fill prescriptions. Union's Bible storybook stained-glass windows were so beautiful folks from all over the South came to Soso to get a look at them.

As loud music filled the air, Johnny Paul looked at Sister Ruby and said, "I ain't never heard such singing rock the walls of a church house in all my born days! Why, it sure does sound like a honky-tonk bar, don't it? Maw, is Johnny Cash in there with his guitar? *Yee-ha!* I betcha a dollar bill ten to one that they all drunk beer with their oatmeal for breakfast like me and Paw did!"

I smiled but wanted to laugh at the floorboard of the Impala.

He burped loudly, and Sister Ruby gave him a sharp whack across the back. He smiled and cried out, "EXCUSE ME!"

When I looked back up, Grandma rolled her eyes at me and was about to speak when Granddaddy cut in with, "This is the day that the Lord hath made. Let us rejoice and be glad in it! Johnny Paul, there's no beer involved!"

Grandma smiled over at him fervently while he quoted bits of Scripture.

I had heard Johnny Paul didn't have a daddy to teach him anything but gambling, drinking, fishing, and storytelling about when he was in the Mississippi State Penitentiary for shooting his own brother, Rudyboy Russell, over a dollar bet on how to spell *Rudolph* one Christmas Eve. His brother put in an *o* where the *u* belonged.

His daddy, Russell Russell, who by the grace of God had landed a job as janitor at the Merchant and Farmer's Bank of Mississippi in Ellisville, was better known for being the town drunk. Everyone at Needles School in Goodlife passed Johnny Paul off as slow, a boy who couldn't learn. Not retarded, but slow. Ignorant. Dumb. A fool even. And after my first and only day there, they made it clear that I was nothing more than white trash and garbage to them as well.

But I knew better. Johnny Paul Russell was more misunderstood, like me, than a fool. We were a lot alike, but in a different way. I couldn't explain it, but I felt connected to him by our aloneness and pain.

"Moonshine corn whiskey then?" Johnny Paul asked, spoken in pure, clear trust that comes before a boy becomes a man.

"No! They are filled with brotherly love," Granddaddy cried out.

"You don't say. I've always wanted me a brother but never knowed I might find one at the church house," he said in a marveling voice. He turned and gave me a wink. I rewarded him with a smile, wondering how beer and oatmeal would taste for breakfast.

Once out of the Impala, I could see into the open church windows. I saw our beloved preacher, Brother Jim Roberts, dancing behind the pulpit to the beat of gospel music led by Sable Farmer, one of Granddaddy's hired hands. The church was filled with voices from Soso, Ellisville, Goshen, Glossolalia, Goodlife, and surrounding neighboring towns along with the voices of those who'd driven over to Soso to see the church's stained-glass windows. Young folks courting would come with picnic lunches on their first date to Soso to see the beautiful storybook windows to make a memory or to get engaged in the lovely churchyard or the adjoining peaceful cemetery. It was normal to see colorful tablecloths spread all over the ground throughout the Soso cemetery on a Sunday afternoon.

From outside I could see folks swaying and singing: *We Shall See the King.*

When we entered the church, Brother Jim Roberts cried out, "I want everyone to shake hands and be friendly! Now be kind to one another! Forget your troubles and yesterday's feuding and fighting amongst yourselves!"

Everyone laughed.

I turned toward a pew with a red ribbon tied at its end. I walked over and offered the right hand of fellowship to my best friend, Margie Anne Roberts. "Greetings, Margie Anne," I said as kind as I could.

"Hey, Myra Boone." And while shaking my hand she bent over and whispered, "Can I go home from church with you today for dinner? Momma is hungover from a night filled with Bass's moonshine and wants to get shed of me. Daddy is going to visit the jailhouse and shut-ins. He'll eat with them. I don't want to go back home today with Momma being like she is to me. She's liable to smash my glasses again. I'm afraid one day she will break my nose! Then, I can't go to Needles. Why, my life would be over if I had to even miss one day of school!"

"I'll ask my grandfolks and let you know in a minute," I told her and moved on deeper into the crowd, never knowing the right words to comfort my best friend while often wondering why she loved going to Needles School so much, especially after seeing the way they treated her.

I saw Johnny Paul Russell out of the corner of my left eye standing near the back door, looking lost and like he might break away and run for home.

I introduced myself to an old lady who asked me, "Miss Myra Boone, do you know what *Myra* means?"

"No."

"Santa Claus," the old lady informed me, eyeing me from head to toe with a great suspicion.

I frowned and said, "Never heard *that* before," before walking back to my pew to join my grandfolks.

The old woman shouted out at me, "Ho ho ho! Merry Christmas!"

"Grandma, can Margie Anne come home with me after church for dinner today?" I asked.

"I don't see why not," she told me. "Your Granddaddy bought enough chicken and okra yesterday at the Better Living Grocery Store to fry for ten people. I hope she likes fried chicken and fried okra."

I gave her a quick hug and ran back to Margie Anne who clapped her hands when I asked, "Do you like fried chicken and fried okra?"

"I love both!" she cried out, pushing her thick glasses back up onto her nose.

"See you after church then," I told her. I tapped her on the shoulder and said, "I'll come and find you." When Margie Anne bent over and kissed me on the cheek, I saw the black and blue bruises on her neck she sported but had tried to hide with a knotted red and purple, double layered chiffon scarf.

Walking back to my seat, I heard her pray, "Thank you, Sweet Jesus, for making a way of escape for me. I'm too weak to go to battle with Momma today. She went and set fire to all my pretty scarves last night. I don't know what I'm going to do about my neck come Monday morning when I have to go to Needles."

One day somebody's going to beat the meanness out of that woman for the way she treats Margie Anne.

Brother Jim Roberts got the order back amongst the people. He called on Sister Anita Brown, the tallest woman—seven feet to be exact—in Soso, to lead us in a worship song.

Because of her extreme height, Sister Anita usually went barefoot. Sunday was no exception. She cried out to the congregation, "The

Bible says that *everything* that hath breath, let it praise the Law'd! What do the Bible say?"

We shouted, "Everything!"

Sable Farmer moved off to the side of the aisle to give her the run of the floor.

"Not just the animals or the earth or the ocean or the rocks, but *everything*!" Sister Anita's voice rang out louder. "Do you all want the Law'd God to call out to the rocks or to the seas or to the volcanoes to sing their praises unto Him because we all are too trifling lazy to open our mouths and offer up praise to a Father who gave up His only begotten son, Jesus Christ, to die for us?"

The crowd cheered, "No!"

Johnny Paul Russell shouted, "Hell no! Hell no! Ain't nary a Russell trifling lazy! That's a damn lie if you've been told so!"

Granddaddy grabbed him by the elbow and said, "*Son*, we don't curse in the Lord's house. *Understand?*"

Johnny Paul nodded, burped, and winked over at me. When I smelled beer and oatmeal on his breath, I gave him no encouragement.

"All right then," Sister Anita went on like there was no tomorrow a-coming. "Up, up, up on your feet! Sing, dance, and shout it out to the Master. *Everything* that hath breath, praise the Law'd!"

The crowd roared, "Amen!"

"You drum and guitar players, let it ring out," she commanded. "Brother Tommy Taylor, let them piano keys dance with all their might. Make 'em walk up the sky straight into the City of Heaven! Sister Shirley Stringer, come on up here to the pulpit and take my hand in yours and help me lift up a praise offering amongst these people who love the Law'd!"

When I glanced over to Granddaddy and Grandma Davis, they both nodded at me to say it was fine in their book to go ahead and take part in the worship service. Everything and everybody in the Union Community Church began to sing, clap, and dance to the gospel song *There Is Power in the Blood* while Brother Tommy Taylor let his fingers do the walking on the pearly white piano keys. Brother Tommy Taylor threw up his right leg and began to hit the piano keys with his heel.

I watched Sable's feet catch spiritual fire and take him into a little dance to put them out. We sang: *Would you be free from the burden of sin? / Would you o'er evil a victory win? / There is pow'r, pow'r, / Wonder-working pow'r, / In the blood of the Lamb; / Three's pow'r, pow'r, / Wonder-working pow'r. / In the precious blood of the Lamb.*

Sister Shirley Stringer's face took on an angelic glow when the musicians rocked the walls with gospel music.

I turned to see Sister Ruby dancing and singing in the spirit and smiling with such joy that nary a soul would even notice that she didn't have a tooth in her head. Her face was beaming beneath her purple hat.

Johnny Paul was standing by her side swaying and rocking in his navy blue cowboy boots, not missing a beat to the music. Both lifted their hands to the sky.

Brother Jim Roberts jumped up and began to preach right where he was standing when Sable Farmer reached down and handed him a corded microphone. He held the microphone in his hands like a spear and began to march around the outside aisle of the church like Joshua did around Jericho while everyone sat down.

Brother Jim told us, "The Bible says over in the book of Psalms, chapter 37, verses 1 through 6, *that David* remained steadfast in the love of God when he wrote, 'FRET NOT thyself because of evildoers, neither be thou envious against the workers of iniquity. For they shall soon be cut down like the grass, and wither as the green herb. Trust in the Lord, and do good; *so* shalt thou dwell in the land, and verily thou shalt be fed…'"

I took note of his words.

"Saints of God, are you with me now?" Brother Jim asked.

Our voices cried back at him like hungry bobcats, "Yes!"

He continued on with, "Verse 4 says, '*Delight thyself also in the Lord; and he shall give thee the desires of thine heart. Commit thy way unto the Lord; trust in him; and he shall bring it to pass. And he shall bring forth thy righteousness as light, and thy judgment as the noonday....*'" He waved his Bible at the crowd and shouted, "GLORY!"

Everyone shouted back, "GLORY!"

"One more time," Brother Jim said.

We shouted, "GLORY!"

"The Lord God said through David for us all to remain steadfast in *His love* and in *our love* for Him. He said, 'FRET NOT,' and now that means don't you fret and cry when you lay down to sleep or wake up alone anymore! And don't you fret and cry when you can't scrape enough money together to make ends meet to feed your family either! The Lord God will send a raven to feed every open mouth of those that serve Him with their whole heart. He did it for his hungry boy Elijah, and the Lord God will do it again for the people down here in South Mississippi, if the need be! Brothers and sisters in the Lord God, do you all hear me?"

We answered, "Amen!"

He asked, "What did the Lord God say?"

We answered, "FRET NOT!"

Dabbing off the sweat from his brow with a handkerchief that Sister Shirley had handed to him in his hour of spiritual need, he asked, "Do you know where I'm coming from?"

The emotions surrounding me were so filled by the power that came with the blood of Jesus Christ that I knew he'd soon be sweating and dripping blood like Jesus had dripped on the Calvary cross right before Mary's eyes.

Old man Ananias, with his questionable skin tone, who was forever bound and cripple in a wheelchair, held up a glowing Bible in one hand and shouted at Brother Jim while waving an American flag with his other hand. "I know where you are coming from! And I know where you've been! You are looking at a war Veteran who has cried many a tear over what could have been but never was to be!"

Brother Jim read on: "'*For they shall soon be cut down like* TALL *grass...*'"

Someone asked, "What does that mean?"

"I am glad you asked. Now, that means that God will take care of your enemies, whatever or whoever they might be. Do you believe it?" he asked us.

"We believe it!" we proclaimed.

"Then, say it like you believe it," he went on.

"We believe it! We believe it! We beeeeeeeliiieeee-ve it!" the crowd answered Brother Jim like he'd jumped down from heaven.

"Who hung the stars and the moon in the sky?" he asked.

Everyone shouted in perfect unison, "The Lord God did!"

"Then, I ask you, is there *anything* too hard for our Lord God?"

We shouted in agreement, "No!"

"Who makes the sun shine? Who makes the birds sing? Who makes the flowers bloom in all their glory?"

Everyone shouted, "The Lord God do! The Lord God do! The Lord God do! The Lord God do it all!"

And with that, Sister Ruby Russell jumped up and threw her purple hat as high as she could into the air and caught it with no one seeming to mind at all.

The light of God was all around Brother Jim. He was glowing and giving off heat. He preached and read on to us, "Brothers and Sisters, David wrote: '*And he shall bring forth thy righteousness as the light, and thy judgment' as what?*'"

"As the noonday!"

"Yeee-ha!" Johnny Paul Russell shouted and clicked the heels of his navy blue cowboy boots together three times while waving his red bandana in the air.

Brother Jim stopped talking and wiped his brow. I looked for blood on his handkerchief, but none was present.

"Amen!" the crowd roared.

"Let me read you one more verse of Scripture."

"Read it! Read it! Read it!"

Brother Jim Roberts said, "King James says over in the book of Matthew, chapter 22 beginning at verse 35, and reading on through verse 40: '*Then one of them, which was a lawyer, asked him a question, tempting him, and saying, Master, which is the great commandment in the law?*'"

Someone confirmed, "Uh huh, a nosey lawyer asked the Master a question!"

Brother Jim read on: "'*Jesus said unto him, Thou shalt love the Lord thy God with all thy heart, and with all thy soul, and with all thy mind. This is the first and great commandment. And the second is like unto it, Thou shalt love thy neighbor as thyself. On these two commandments hang all the law and the prophets.*'"

Someone cried out, "A tempting lawyer tried to trip the Master up!"

Granddaddy Davis frowned.

"What do we have to do for our *neighbor?*" Brother Jim asked us.

Voices shouted throughout the sanctuary, "Love him!"

Brother Jim softly said, "Always love your neighbor as yourself. Love. You must go find folks to love—no matter what! No s-e-x-involved! Love is the key that unlocks the gate to the City of Heaven and all the worlds without end—known and unknown! Love can turn the evil heart of mankind to good. You can't give up on the promises of God, let alone loving your neighbors, who are pretty much like you unto yourselves!"

Standing, Brother Tommy Taylor made the piano sprout legs and walk.

Brother Jim threw his hands into the sky and made his request known to God, "Sweet Jesus, call us to our heavenly home right now if it be Thy will! Make us angels in Glory!"

Everyone jumped up like it was going to happen.

Sister Shirley grabbed hold of Sister Anita's free hand. She had a tambourine in her other hand. Both women ran to the altar and began to dance before it.

They are sure a sight to see!

I turned around and saw that Johnny Paul Russell had strayed off and was standing up on the ledge of the stained-glass storybook window that told the story of Jonah from Nineveh in the whale's belly. Johnny Paul Russell was looking out the window. Then, without warning and while waving his red bandana, he jumped right out of the whale's belly.

I screamed and pointed, "Johnny Paul Russell jumped out of the window with Jonah in the whale's belly!"

Granddaddy Davis jumped up from his pew and took off leading the way outside with everyone close at his heels. Once we got outside the church house and found Johnny Paul Russell, who was brushing off his navy blue cowboy boots, Granddaddy asked him, "Johnny Paul, what in the world did you mean by jumping out the church house window? Son, what *were* you thinking?"

"I was thinking that I love my paw! And I ain't aiming to go nowhere without him! When that preacher man asked Sweet Jesus to call us to our Heavenly home and make us angels in Glory, I knew right then, I couldn't go nowhere, not even to the City of Heaven, without my paw, so I jumped before Jesus called my name. Heck fire, I'm the only friend besides his drinking partner Everett Bass that Paw has left. Paw's only brother got shot on account of a family misunderstanding between them about an old reindeer at Christmastime, you know, right? That's why we never get any presents from family for Christmas."

Granddaddy looked confounded. Speechless. He bent over and helped Johnny Paul Russell dust himself off before picking him up and giving him a big hug. Finally, while looking at the church window and back to Johnny Paul Russell, Granddaddy said, "Son, you did the right thing. Your Paw would be proud of you for jumping out of that whale's belly!"

Johnny Paul Russell beamed, stuck his chest out, tipped his cowboy hat, and said, "Thank you kindly, Sir." Then, he folded his bandana in the shape of a red diamond and placed it into Granddaddy's shirt pocket like a handkerchief and shouted, "FRET NOT!"

Granddaddy Davis nodded and smiled at him.

The more I thought about Johnny Paul Russell's words, the more I believed him not ignorant at all. That boy wasn't about to leave his Paw behind with the rest of the sinners of this world even if he was one of the biggest.

After we said our goodbyes to our church friends, I went back inside to fetch Margie Anne Roberts. She was on her knees, black and blue as ever, gaining strength in the prayer room. When I searched the prayer room for another familiar face, I found it as empty as a dry well. When I offered Margie Anne a helping hand to stand, she took it and I helped her to her feet.

"Margie Anne, I'll see if I can find you a pretty chiffon scarf or two at Magnolia Sunday to take home with you to wear to Needles tomorrow. Would that ease your mind some?" I asked her.

"Oh, yes, Myra! I would love a new scarf or two!"

Then, happily smiling and gently holding my ugly hands, my best friend and I walked to the Impala to join my grandfolks and Sister Ruby and Johnny Paul Russell.

While driving back to Magnolia Sunday, Johnny Paul Russell told us spiritual and mystical stories found deep within the Piney Woods. Granddaddy Davis stopped at Blue's Corner Store for some ice-cold soft drinks for everyone to enjoy. Then, Granddaddy fulfilled his promise to his beloved white-faced collie jewels, Jack and Jill. He got a Pepsi-Cola with two cups of ice cubes making sure he didn't leave anyone, man, or beast, thirsty for love or anything thing else on that Sunday in May.

PARADISE

Chapter 15

ONE OF THE BEST THINGS about living at Magnolia Sunday with my grand folks was going to town. We made the drive to the neighboring town of Ellisville every Saturday without fail to shop for store-bought food for the week ahead. Grandma Reatha liked to call me "Child" instead of my given name. I soon realized that I was her favorite person because she used to slip me a dollar every Saturday morning before we loaded up Granddaddy's Impala to hit the road early to beat the heat.

Pressing a crunched-up picture of George Washington into the palm of my hand, Grandma Reatha told me, "Child, now don't you go tell none of the rest of them. Do you hear me?"

I showed her she could trust me by nodding my head, then think to myself *Thank You Lord,* while remembering I had to give Him a dime of my good fortune come Sunday morning.

Grandma got up early to make us plenty of road snacks like scrambled egg sandwiches, figs, and biscuits and syrup. The trip took about an hour and a half depending on us stopping and looking at interesting roadside sites and such along the way.

Stopping under the only red light in Ellisville, I remember looking over at the Jones County Courthouse and seeing the water fountains out in front that were marked "White" and "Colored."

I asked Grandma, "What do you reckon the good Lord thinks about them water fountains?"

She replied, "Now you hush, Child, because there ain't nary thing you can do about it anyway, so you sit back and stay quiet afore somebody hears you and comes out to Magnolia Sunday and burns one of them devil crosses in our front yard for the whole Union Community to see."

Granddaddy Spurgeon interrupted while holding up a sack and asked, "How about a fig?"

I'd hold tight onto my dollar while remembering my momma's face and search my memory as if my mind held within it some sort of an answer for what I knew at the tender age of twelve was nothing but the disregard for people.

"Well," I said, reaching into the sack to get me a big, ripe juicy fig, "if my daddy was alive, he wouldn't let none of them burn those devil crosses in our front yard! And I bet he'd take a hammer and bust up those water fountains and be a *hero* all over the state of Mississippi! Why, even President John F. Kennedy would call him to Washington, D. C., to the White House for a medal or something."

Granddaddy shouted, "That girl has a mind of her own—twelve going on twenty-four!"

We laughed and rode on to Blue's Corner Store for a cold soft drink before going to the Better Living Grocery Store.

"Who wants an ice-cold Coca-Cola? How about you, Reatha?" Granddaddy asked.

"Not me. I want a 10-2-4—a Dr. Pepper!" Grandma said enthusiastically.

"How about you, Lover Girl?"

I laughed and requested an Orange Crush which was once my daddy's favorite. He'd oblige me with great pleasure while we shared the unspoken secret that we were happy because each of us had requested a different kind of cold soft drink. Now we could share in a little taste of our once-a-week pleasure of a store-bought flavored soft drink. A mighty fine time we were having. Being together was enough to make us smile. No one had to ask us if we were having fun because we were smiling like showy blue morning glories outside a fence on a county road right about sunrise while we ate our scrambled egg sandwiches on Little Miss Sunbeam White Bread while a sipping on our cold soft drinks sitting in the shade hoping a cool breeze would soon join us.

Now Blue's Corner Store is the most wonderful place you can ever imagine. Old Man Blue has a talking parrot named Lester. Everyone for miles around talked about Lester. Why, even some families spent of all their Saturday afternoon sitting under the big mimosas eating watermelon and cracking pecans, discussing Old Man Blue's talking bird. The main thing about Lester was that he could talk and make perfect sense. He was as smart as a horse. He knew everyone in the entire Union Community by name. Even if you walked in and he had his back turned to you, the minute you said, "Orange Crush, please," Lester looked over towards the register and said as plain as day, "That'll be ten cents, Miss Myra." Then, he gave a one-syllable sharp and to-the-point whistle while raising his right foot at you to wave you onward.

And like a proud father, Old Man Blue smiled and said, "That Lester, if it wasn't for him, I couldn't keep up with the price of things!"

I was sure that one day someone from Hollywood would come into Blue's Corner Store, by accident of course, looking for the city of Goodlife and steal Lester and break all our hearts. We loved him so. He was our brightest star.

After we shared a few minutes with Old Man Blue and Lester and whoever else might have been in the store, we headed on over to the center of town. We circled around the stores two or three times trying to get a parking space in the front so we could see everyone coming in and out of the store. Then, we'd all pile out of the Impala and head for town.

Although it was supposed to be a happy trip for us, and for the most part it was, it also saddened my heart to look around me in what was supposed to be known as a "free country" called America and see such goings on as I witnessed in the small town of Ellisville. But in 1962, I saw no freedom in South Mississippi. What I saw in front of the Better Living Grocery Store and lining the town streets were old pickup trucks and rusty old cars, and in them sat some of the Colored women and their children. Now I am sure they would have loved to have gone in to shop for the week like I was so *freely* allowed to go in with my grand folks.

After all, everyone looked forward to Saturday for that reason alone—going to town. It didn't take a twelve-year-old orphan to figure out that there was not much fun in going to town if you had to sit in the car *outside* of the store once you got there instead of going on *inside*.

What do the white folks mean by not letting the Colored woman and their children go inside the store like the rest of us?

As I walked along the sidewalks towards the center of Ellisville on Appletree Street, I saw the looks on their faces—like someone had reached into their chests and jerked out their hearts before they ever had a chance to become what God had intended them to be. Each person had the same look, the look of love like my momma had on her face when she would so sing to me along with Ray Charles on the box radio *You Are My Sunshine* before she flew Home, to Heaven, with Daddy and Great Aunt Annabelle.

Walking past the Colored folks, I felt like I was a sparrow alone on a housetop with nothing but a mean old owl circling around me waiting for his chance to swoop down upon my slender body and leave nothing of me on this old earth but a bag of bones like they found when they discovered my folks and my great aunt had been burned slam up in the house fire that December night. Three bags of bones were all that was left of the only three people that I had ever loved. The Boones, except for me, were bones on account of me.

Bags of bones were not enough to satisfy the broken heart I would carry with me for the rest of my life as well as having the thoughts of losing them at such an early age. I blamed myself. Every day in Goodlife, I'd remember when we buried what was left of the two people who I still loved with all my heart in those green, velvet-lined wooden boxes in the family cemetery right outside of the Union Community Church in Soso. That concrete statue of Jesus Christ that my grandfolks had put on top of their grave with the Bible in His hands didn't comfort me all the time like they'd hope it would either. But just the same, I was glad Jesus was there to watch over their bones.

It was in the Union Cemetery in Soso where I first felt a measure of peace, not in the church house or any house, for that matter. Then, it was amid the tender grass outside the House of Joy and Life when Enoch Vine and I had watched the clouds float over our heads that I knew peace within my soul was possible. And I had felt as rich as cream. I knew I had to get my courage up and to some way, somehow tell my grandfolks like Enoch had suggested about what I believed to be true about the house fire. The truth wasn't going to be easy.

We went to church more than most because it was our main way to socialize with others except for Colored folks. It was in town where I saw the Colored folks who worked hard tending the fields all week long the same as the rest of the community did. It didn't seem right to me that they couldn't enjoy simple things like shopping for food together, drinking from the same water fountain, eating in the front of the diner, and sitting up front in a church house like me and my grandfolks did at the funeral. There was nothing I could do about it.

Suddenly, what Momma had always told me to do when I had nobody to talk to save for her and Daddy and Great Aunt Annabelle, *Just write*, popped into my head. I went back to the car and searched for some writing paper. I sat down right then and there and wrote the Lord God a letter. It was my first letter since the house fire. It was all I knew to do, *Just write*, no matter what. The pain in my ugly hands never entered my mind while writing.

May 30, 1962

Dear Lord God,

I love You.

Thank You for all my many blessings, even though I don't always count them. I am especially grateful because I believe I will see my folks one day when You call me to the City of Heaven to be with You and them. Just one thing, please don't make me sing with the Angels because the only two people I know who could or can sing was my momma and Ray Charles. Please let me see him one day, if it's not too much trouble, so I can ask him to sing You Are My Sunshine to me. But the real reason for this letter is because I am so sad to see these Colored folks of Yours having to suffer here in Ellisville. I know that I am only twelve, but if You give me the power in some way or another, I promise You I will help these mighty fine Colored people.

Lord, let all of us, one day, love one another like You said in the Bible over in the book of John: "'A new commandment I give unto you, That ye love one another; as I have loved you, that ye also love one another. By this shall all men know that ye are my disciples, if ye have love one to another'." John 13:34-35 is my memory verse for the month of May at the Union Community Church in Soso.

Most everybody has got seeds to sow. Don't these Colored folks have so very much to sow? I can see it in their faces. Their souls are hurting because they have so much to sow, and nobody will let them. They are on the outside looking in. But wouldn't it be better if they went on in, and then were able to look out, like the rest of us? Please, help us to understand that our walk and our talk must go along together.

I thank You for the Union Community Church in Soso. I ask You to some way or the other to fix it so we can all be together because I know You are not a color. You are a Light.

It doesn't make much difference to me how long You take to answer this letter just so You answer it in time. I believe You are with me. And I'm listening as best as I know how.

Love,
Mary "Myra" Boone
Goodlife, Mississippi 39437

I folded up my letter so I could put it in my Bible as soon as we got back to Magnolia Sunday, believing one day God would answer it. Then, I went on into town to shop and spend my ninety cents.

"MYRA, WHY, THERE'S Miss Lula Lane, Elisha Pearl, and Lazina

LaRue," Grandma observed as we approached one of the old trucks filled with Colored folks.

"How ya'll doin'?" Lula Lane asked us.

"We fine. How you?" Grandma asked them.

Granddaddy took off his hat, fanned his face, and said, "It hot enough for you?"

"We findin' it as hots as fire!" one of them cried out and wiped the sweat from her forehead before clearing her throat and spitting out the truck window.

Lula had a small child propped up on a wooden crate sitting beside her who began to bawl. "What time has you got, Mister Davis?"

Looking at his gold pocket watch, "It's pretty near nine-thirty or so," Granddaddy replied.

Reaching for her bawling child, Lula said, "Why, I do declare it's pretty near time for my Ballou to be a-gittin' it on back to the truck. Now hush up, Babydoll. Now hush."

"Good Gaw'd Almighty! If our men ain't slower than the seven-year itch, I don't know who is!" Elisha Pearl cried out.

Waving to a child who appeared to be a little girl with root beer brown skin and hazel eyes, I asked, "It is hot, isn't it? How long have you all been waiting?" The little girl was as beautiful as the sound of a gospel song.

"I reckon pretty near two hour or longer," Lula replied.

"What's her name?" Grandma asked Lula.

"This here's Eunice. Her name means *happy*. I got it out of the *Life* magazine when I was cleaning Mister Ed Reynolds' mansion, White Shadow."

"Can you read?" I asked.

"Just a little on account of never been schooled like you," she said sheepishly. She smiled and twitched her left shoulder up at me.

"Shoot! That's what you think, but it isn't so. I didn't start first grade until I was twelve!" I reached into the truck window to pat her on the arm and whispered soft and low, "And truth be told, I quit the selfsame day."

The others giggled.

One of them said soft and low, "Girly Girl, you lie about school."

"Know what *Life* magazine means?" one of them asked me.

"Why, no. What?" I replied

"Where there's *Life*, there's hope," she told me, smiling all the while.

The others giggled.

The same Colored girl repeated herself soft and low, "Girly Girl, you lie about school."

Remembering I had some money in my pocket to spend, I said, "Shush! No, I'm not! Hey, you all want a cold soft drink?"

In a marveling voice with eyes as wide as the Mississippi River, one of them asked, "Has you got an icebox with you in that there right fine gold car?"

Noticing the other Colored folks watching us from their car windows, I still said, "Why, no! But I got a dollar bill right here."

The three of them looked from one to the other, then back to me.

Lula punched Elisha Pearl to speak up, so she whispered, "We would if you dare buy."

"Do we get to pick?" Lazina asked, stepping out of the truck. Her countenance changed when some cooler air hit her face.

"Of course! How else would I know what you wanted? Do I look like a mind reader?" I replied.

When Eunice laughed at my voice, I heard another cry from the back seat.

"Myra, are you sure you want the other town folks to see you buying them a cold soft drink?" Grandma whispered to me.

I nodded. "I'm sure."

While Granddaddy watched me close, I saw his eyes get misty, which made me think I was doing the right thing—what he wanted to do but wouldn't or couldn't or both. I realized that sometimes God's love was shown to others in secret. And I knew since I'd come to live with them at Magnolia Sunday, he'd had a hard time saying no to me for anything. I was counting on this time not being any different.

Handing Eunice to Elisha Pearl, Lula said, "That's Eunice's sister, Susie Q."

I knew I was right when Granddaddy spoke up and said, "Now hold on a minute before you ladies get to jabbering! Tell me what kind of cold soft drinks that you all want. I will step into George Wilkerson's drugstore and get us all one."

Bouncing Susie Q. as steady as possible on her hip, Lula said, "NuGrape."

"Diet-Rite Sugar Free Cola. I've got a touch of the *Sugar Diabetes*," Lazina said.

"A Frostie Root Beer!" Elisha Pearl shouted.

Granddaddy turned and headed towards the drugstore, forgetting my dollar bill and leaving us womenfolk to talk. When he returned with their cold soft drinks, Elisha Pearl reached for her Frostie and shouted, "Why, bless your big ol' heart, Mister Davis!"

"Thank you, a plenty!" one of them cried out.

"Amen," Lula shouted, NuGrape in hand.

"Did you get to see the picture postal cards that George Wilkerson has posted throughout his drugstore of North Carolina and that Duke University?" Lulu asked Granddaddy.

George Wilkerson had named his drugstore "Eruditio et Religio" because he intended it to be a place of compassion and more than a place for medicine. He'd name his drugstore for what he came to believe was true about life that book knowledge mixed with faith being the two keys to opening anyone's mind. It didn't seem to bother George that folks couldn't pronounce its name. In fact, I didn't know of anyone in Goodlife or Ellisville or Soso who could say the name like George could. He didn't care though. He said that would give them a chance to learn something new; otherwise, they'd get stale like old bread in their thinking. And no one liked stale bread not even Lester.

Everyone loved George because as far as everyone was concerned, he was "well-travelled" and kind and big-hearted. He'd been out of Mississippi when most of us hadn't been any further than the town of Ellisville or the Mississippi State Capitol in Jackson. George was loyal to his customers, and everyone was loyal to him. He was widely known for having a good heart and thought highly of for giving extra refills to broke poor folks who couldn't get back in to see their doctor for one reason or the other. He also had been known to give out an amulet or two to the dying. Right or wrong, that's the way it was. And besides, everyone who came to town loved to hear him tell stories about his North Carolina days *and* nights from Durham to Chapel Hill while he was attending Duke University. He had even driven through the Great Smoky Mountains National Park in North Carolina and Tennessee, where some fellow named Rockefeller helped buy.

"Yes, I did see some picture postal cards. Why?" Granddaddy replied to Lulu.

"I dream about going inside Mister George's drugstore even if I can't say its name right and spend as long as he'll let me look at his picture postal cards of North Carolina and that Duke University Chapel with those fancy stained-glass storybook windows everyone talks about. I dream about seeing what a bonafide university looks like. I want Eunice to see too. I want her to have a purpose in life. I want her to have bettern' me. I want her to have hope. That's why I asked you. I hope Mister George don't take them down until my dream comes true," Lulu told us.

Bending forward, I told her, "I hope your dream comes true."

Lulu smiled at me and did a little happy dance while bouncing her head from side-to-side. We left the Colored women in their old truck all smiling and dreaming of better days and the hope that comes with the stories told on picture postal cards of North Carolina. They were content to cool off with their cold soft drinks until their hard-working Colored menfolk returned to their sides.

ON MY WAY BACK TO THE IMPALA, I looked over towards the Ellisville courthouse and saw a crowd of folks huddled under a large sign that read: *France* not too far from the water fountains labeled *White* and *Colored.* Beneath the large sign was a smaller sign that read:

Sparrows: 5 *Cents Each. Buy Two & Get One Free.*

Granddaddy Spurgeon called out, "Myra, come meet Bucky Stringer, the *Birdman.*"

I walked towards the crowd and an old Colored man.

"Myra, meet Bucky Stringer. Bucky Stringer, meet Myra Boone. Bucky is selling sparrows. He catches them during the week and puts them in these big colorful cages for his neighboring farmers and the local merchants to buy on Saturday in case they don't make it to church come Sunday," Granddaddy informed me.

Observing that he had no feet, I said, "Howdy, Mister Stringer."

He looked at me with the face of the earth and shouted, "Pleased to make your acquaintance, *Madam Myra Boone!*"

"Glad to meet you too!" I shouted back.

When Mister Stringer saw me staring at his nubs, he explained, "I lost both my feet in World War II. Didn't get nary a Medal of Honor or me a Purple Heart Medal for it though. But I am the only Colored Southerner who shook the left hand of a very hot-headed Winston Churchill before he was left alone to fight in the Battle of Britain right about... Ohohoh early July 1940, to Uhuuhu the end of October 1940 or so. Ain't got no family either, so I gots to make me a dollar the best way I know how. Would you like to buy a sparrow, Madam Myra?"

Looking at Granddaddy, I asked, "What for?"

Grandma Reatha was standing in a long line of folks chatting away while others were putting their spare change and dry goods into a big bucket near Bucky Stringer's wheelchair.

"Why, for praying and wishing, of course!" Mister Stringer cried out. When a feeble-minded-looking girl joined us, he said, "Madam Myra, this here is Virgie. She looks after me."

"Hey, Virgie," I said.

"Hey, back!" Virgie cried out.

"My wife ran off after our only boy, Bolt, died after he was tarred and feathered a while back," he told me.

Frowning, I turned and walked towards three big bird cages. One was green, one was yellow, and one was blue. The blue cage was four feet tall and had a shiny streak of yellow paint outlining its little red door that was latched by a long safety pin. Over the door was a tiny green sign that read: *Caen, France, Battle of Normandy, 1944*. On all three of the bird cages was a sign reading: *God's eye is on the sparrow. And I know He loves me. Buy 2!*

When I spotted a sick small sparrow that was hunkered down in the back of the yellow cage, I told Bucky, "Mister Stringer, I'll take that one."

Smiling, Bucky Stringer wheeled himself over to the yellow cage. Once he caught sight of the bird I'd chosen, he shouted, "Ohohoh, that's a right finnn-e one! Ohohoh, yes, Madam Myra, I do like *that* one!"

I offered him a nickel for the sparrow, and he took it. While he was struggling with the door's safety pin, I noticed the back of his truck was loaded with cardboard boxes packed slam full of dry goods. I saw a sack of cornmeal, a five-pound bucket of lard, a box of Kellogg's Corn Flakes, a block of dry ice, fresh brown hen eggs, a big cake of homemade lye soap, a slab of bacon, a bushel of snap beans and a box wrapped with Christmas paper that held a heap of mixed fruit.

Towards the front of the truck's cab was a carton for Frostie Root Beer, a sack of dry dog food, and even a box of Morton Salt with a dangling price tag of 3-cents off to the side of a girl holding umbrella taking a salt shower. She had yellow plaited pigtails.

I felt something jerking at my heart, so I reached into my pocket and brought back a quarter and said, "Mister Stringer, if you don't mind, I'll take five more sparrows, please."

Bucky's face lit up like the sun, and he said with a little hint of a French accent, "Wewe, wewe, wewe, wewe, wewe, Madam Myra!"

Grandma walked up and told him, "Bucky, give me the one with the white streak running straight down the middle of its back."

"Glad to oblige," he replied. He gave me the once-over and said, "My, my, my, you look *exotic*. Are you from Mexico? You got pretty skin."

I laughed.

Virgie mimicked me.

Holding up a dime, Granddaddy told him, "And I reckon I'll take two."

"Don't forget you get a *free* one when you *buy* two," Bucky reminded him.

Virgie spoke up and asked, "How many does Myra get free with six?"

Bucky blared out, "Four!"

Granddaddy frowned.

Again, I laughed.

Virgie walked over to Granddaddy and asked, "Mister, may I have your free one? I ain't aiming to go to church tomorrow. The good Lord knows I'm in need of more patience tending this fool old man who even talks in his sleep about a Mister Winston Churchill!"

"Go on. Take it," he told her.

Virgie clapped her hands together in excitement.

I noticed Grandma had sneaked off away from the crowd and that she was stroking her sparrow's white streak. I saw her shade her eyes and look up into the sky while shaking her head three times before blowing once on the sparrow. And as she raised her hands above her head to set the bird free, she shouted, "God bless ugly Ike!"

"Tell us about France," a voice from the crowd cried out.

Grandma rejoined us and said, "Come on, let's head on back to Magnolia Sunday."

"If I would have learned to *read and write* and not quit school before I went off to fight in World War II, why, I wouldn't be here a-selling sparrows today!" Bucky Stringer shouted. We were surrounded by hot laughter from the crowd. Once the laughter cooled down, I welcomed Granddaddy's hand in mine and became happy to let him escort me to the Impala with Grandma at our heels, all the while reminding us that Bucky Stringer quit school before he went off to fight in World War II and that he had no feet but only God's precious little sparrows and faithful prayers of the Saints—some living; some dead to keep him company for the rest of his life because even a feeble-minded girl like Virgie could one day run out of nickels, dimes, and patience and disappear to fight in her own battle.

ON THE WAY TO MAGNOLIA SUNDAY, we passed the Jones Home for Boys. That is when Granddaddy Spurgeon started to tell the most famous story he would ever tell. "It was in a boy's home like that one there where they *hid* Ray Charles Robinson away when he was a boy."

Sitting up straight to listen, I asked him, "You know about *that*?"

"Sure, I know. See, Ray Charles was not born blind, only poor and Colored and a Robinson to boot. It was the height of the Depression years. They had to hit the road running early on because his birth was a surprise. Aretha Robinson, his maw, had nothing but the ground beneath her. Compared to other Colored folks, she and Ray were on the bottom of the ladder looking up at everyone else. Aretha was an orphan herself. She was born a Williams. The Robinson's adopted her, so to speak, when she was a teenager."

Grandma Reatha looked uncomfortable.

"How in the world do you know all this?" I asked.

"Well, Ray's maw, Aretha, and I stacked boards at Shorty Hilton's sawmill when we weren't working the fields getting in crops. She never spoke of his Poppa. We all did odd jobs in a district of western Florida. At one time, they lived in the community of Jellyroll. Jellyroll was a bad place to have to live, let alone raise children. All that was before I worked the Mississippi fields and picked her cotton. That's how I know it," he answered as if he was a celebrity.

Grandma looked over at him and smiled, claiming him as hers while she bounced in the front seat as we hit a bunch of potholes in the road. She commented, "Spurgeon Davis, you were a poor boy yourself stuck in Greenville, Florida, until you rode a horse down to Mississippi and settled in Goodlife to work the fields."

One thing I know for sure was my granddaddy was never ashamed of working the fields as a boy be it a cotton, a watermelon, or a cantaloupe field. He believed hard work was God's will for his life. He was right proud of it.

He continued the story. "Aretha would come to the bonfire in front of Shorty Hilton's sawmill. Shorty was one of the richest men in the state of Florida. We'd gather to warm up early about 4:30 every morning. It didn't take a fool to know she was troubled about something. It was Ray. He was beginning to pass from light into darkness at the age of four. Aretha would sing and pray all day for the boy. But it was fate, I guess. Because by the time Ray was six or seven, he was about blind."

"What about his daddy? Why didn't he take him up to the Florida State Hospital? Why didn't they take him to the church for the folks to anoint him with the olive oil and pray the prayer of faith? Why didn't somebody *do* something?" I cried out.

"Now Myra, don't you go getting upset. Do you hear me?" Grandma said and rolled down her window a little so I could get some cool air blowing in on my face.

I sat back for fear she would make him stop the story, and so I said, "I ain't."

Granddaddy Spurgeon nodded and continued on with, "Because Ray Charles Robinson was a Colored orphan. That's why. And it wasn't as easy as it is now for Colored folks. Aretha once told me what hurt Ray the most was even at the Saint Augustine charity home for the deaf and blind, they separated the Whites and Coloreds. Ray, like your daddy, Virgil, was a charity student. If it hadn't of been for your daddy riding him around and all, they both might have died of loneliness."

In amazement I cried out, "You know about *that* too?"

"Sure, I do," he told me.

Remembering the stories of Ray Charles Robinson my folks had told me in Meridian, I felt my heart flitter and my eyes grow wide before I asked, "What about his Maw? Couldn't she get him out and bring him home?"

Grandma Reatha hung her head down but didn't speak.

"Ray's maw, Aretha, did the best she knew how, praying night and day. I'm sure of it. She had to put him in a boy's home because she had to work the fields. At one time or another, Ray and his maw both worked as sharecroppers. It was harder to tend to Ray and work the field on account of his blindness. Besides, she knew he would learn a trade. Ray learned Braille and to type as well as how to weave some of the finest baskets you ever laid your eyes on. That is where he discovered mathematics and its correlation to music. He learned to compose and arrange music in his head—the hard way—telling and feeling out the parts, one by one. It turned out that he held seven years of what they call *sight memory* like colors, things of the backwoods country, and his maw's face—way back in the far corners of his mind."

"Like me, Granddaddy?"

"Like you what?"

"I remember Momma's face. And I remember when my daddy used to let me sit on his lap in the cool of sundown as the sky turned from blue to pink to purple, then to black, and I would eat raisins. The ones that come in the red box with the sunshine over the Indian's head. I surely did!"

We all laughed.

"If you knew Ray Charles from way back and that Daddy and Ray were friends, then why didn't you like it when Momma and Daddy got married?" I asked them.

Neither spoke for what seemed like a week or more, then it was Grandma who said, "Myra, it was my fault. I made a mistake. A big mistake—the kind you can't take back no matter what you do, say, or pray. I've never confessed it to anyone, not even your Granddaddy, let alone to the good Lord, until now."

Granddaddy cut his eyes at her but didn't say a word. Instead, he reached over and put his arm around her when she wailed out, "And I want to tell you both right now that I am sorry from the bottom of my heart! I am so, so, so sorry I didn't respect Marigold's decision to marry Virgil Boone and lost out on all those years with her. And you!"

My eyes widened. I didn't know what to do or say. It may have been a good time to tell them both my mistake—an even bigger mistake than Grandma had made—killing the only three people that had ever loved me, but I couldn't get the words out of my mouth. Instead of saying 'I'm so, so, so sorry too,' I leaned forward and patted Grandma Reatha on the shoulder like Paula had patted me at the Opportunity House. She rested her old, wrinkled face on my young, ugly hand. When her tears came, they felt like cement bonding us together by a love that we both shared for Momma. For a mile or so, no one said anything until Granddaddy went on telling the most famous story he knew.

"There was a family who had a box radio in Madison County, Florida. Sharecroppers walked for miles every Saturday night to hear the Grand Ole Opry on it. They also played and danced to the beat of their own music. If you want to know the truth about it, we poor folks sang and danced to everything anyone and everyone played. Eventually, they brought Ray. I believe that's when he was getting his *calling* right out in our front yard under a big pecan tree. I can still see him in my mind—smiling and bobbing his head from side-to-side on that Florida dirt road while listening to music. Those were some of the best times of my life, do you hear me? I hated to see Ray and his blindness as much as the rest of the community did. You must always remember that we don't know *why* the Lord God does things the way He does sometimes, but, Lover Girl, you always remember He does everything for a reason and with a purpose in mind," Granddaddy told me.

"And sometimes the Lord God isn't the one doing things, other folks are!" Grandma put in.

"Amen to that," he said

"What's a *calling*?" I asked.

"Well, it's what the Lord God puts in your heart that nobody can take it out no matter what they say, do, or don't do for you or to you. Your *calling* stays until you die. You die called," he told me.

I am lucky to be in the same car, let alone living with such two wise people.

My Granddaddy Davis was one of the best, if not *the* best, storyteller in the state of Mississippi. Everybody knew that for sure. I had no reason to doubt a single word he said. It didn't matter to me if his version of Ray Charles' story was the same as Momma's or Daddy's version either. After all, some stories are told for their truths while others are told to entertain and to pass the time away. In the South, our stories are told for both.

Grandma said, "The Lord's *calling* is what Hollywood folks try to call talent. A calling isn't something you learn. It's something you do natural-like almost without trying like washing your hands under cool running water any time of any day of any week of any year."

I smiled, knowing what she meant. Granddaddy nodded his head in agreement as the Impala lulled us into a satisfied mood along the country roads out of Ellisville on to Goodlife bonded by our mistakes.

WE WERE ALMOST at Magnolia Sunday when we stopped at Lloyd Calhoun's shack out by Taylor Creek. I felt as sorry for the Florida-born Calhoun family as I did for the Mississippi-born chickens I tended in the hen house because there were seven Calhouns living in two rooms crowded up together like my chickens—all waiting for something to happen. With one room being the kitchen and the other being the bedroom, I figured that they must have to wake up and to go to bed at the same time. Otherwise, they'd never get any shut-eye. If it was cold weather, they all would be sitting around the wood-burning stove in the kitchen like there was no tomorrow coming trying to keep from freezing slam to death. But thank goodness for May's warm weather because some of them were all piled up on the front porch shelling butterbeans to put up for the winter.

As soon as we drove up the path, three of them boys took to running towards the Impala yelling, "Git on out here quick, Ma. We's gots company driving up the path to visit!"

They were as happy to see us as if we had been the preacher man coming around in the middle of the week to visit toting a bag of fresh fruit.

"Is your paw home?" Granddaddy asked the three boy—Weber, Marvin, and Babe. All three boys were running and whooping towards the car like they hadn't ever seen one before or at least in quite some time, I figured.

"Why, no. He went up to the Reynolds' Place to tend the north watermelon field. They is about ripe enough to load up and be took to Jackson to sell. He got shed of us with these here butterbeans. Ain't they mighty fine? Big Boys. All the way from Selma, Alabama, brung to us by Aunt Jenny, our Ma's baby sister," one of them said.

The biggest boy, Weber, said, "Mister Davis, has you got your gold watch with you?"

Reaching into the front pocket of his britches, then pulling out the watch his daddy had given him from the old Southern Railroad, Granddaddy said, "I suppose I do."

Once the Colored boys gathered around to see it, their Ma yelled and got results, "Git on back up on the porch and finish shelling these Big Boys with your sisters a-fore your Paw gets home and finds ya'll gathered around a watch like it is a sweet potato pie or something!"

Slapping the top of his britches leg while shaking his head, Marvin said, "Mister Davis, heck fire, I swear I will have me one of them gold watches one ah these days."

Shaking his head in amazement at his brothers who were grinning, Babe said, "Gosh dog! It shore be fine, ain't it?"

"I said git on back up on the porch. Right now! Ya'll hear me?" Lucy Calhoun yelled out.

The soulful sound of Lucy's voice made me smile.

Ignoring the boys for a minute while they got settled once again on the front porch with their pans of butterbeans, Lucy asked us, "What's your testimony?"

"Not much new to tell, neighbor," Grandma replied.

"Oh?" Lucy asked.

Reaching into the back seat for a sack, "We went into Ellisville to shop. I got you a little something from the Better Living Grocery Store," she told Lucy.

With Grandma's words, all five of them Calhoun children jumped right back up and took to running towards the Impala and spilling their pans of butterbeans all over the steps of the front porch. They about give me a heart attack, not to mention giving their Ma one too.

"Weber, Marvin, Babe, Oprah, and Aretha, git on back up here and pick up your butterbeans!" Lucy yelled out.

"Oh, Lucy, Lord have mercy, let them have a little fun," Grandma told her and proceeded to pull out Georgia peaches, brown hen eggs, a sugar-cured ham, a bunch of mustard greens, a slab of salt pork meat, and some peppermints from the sack. "Now these are for your Sunday dinner. Lucy, you are always doing so much for the ladies at the Wednesday prayer meeting with all your needlework and blessing us with your singing. Face it, you've got the prettiest voice in Goodlife."

"The voice of an angel, Paw says. I heard him say it about a hundred times," Weber said.

Smiling, the others nodded their heads and waited for their peppermints.

"Oh, go on, Miss Reatha. There ain't nary a bit of truth in what you say. I use what the good Lord give me to use is all. He be the one

Who blesses it. To tell the truth, I'm right thankful to get out on Wednesday night and away from this wild bunch of mine. You all is as good as gold to let an old black body like me sneak in and join ya'll," Lucy told her.

Granddaddy began giving out peppermints to the children. They were about as happy as newborn pups eating for the first time. He reached into the glove compartment of the Impala and pulled out a little brown sack. "This is for Lloyd. It's a can of Prince Albert and a pack of rolling papers in case he's short this month."

Marveling at the store-bought tobacco, Marvin said, "*Shoot a squirrel for Sunday dinner!* Would ya jud'st look at that there silver-red can with a man in a Sunday suit on it?"

"Thank you kindly. Why, you folks are mighty kind neighbors to me. That's all I know. Can I get you a mess of Big Boys?" Lucy asked us.

"AllthewayfromSelmaAlabama!" Weber yelled across the front yard without taking a breath. He had wandered off to eat his peppermint candy alone so he could enjoy it all by himself. But he still wanted us to know that he was keeping an eye on things, or us.

"No, but I thank you kindly. We got to be getting on back to Magnolia Sunday before it gets completely dark," Grandma replied.

When Lucy saw me in the back seat eating the last of the biscuits and syrup Grandma Reatha had packed for us to eat, she called out, "Is that little Myra? My land sakes alive, she's as pretty as a picture. What's she doing so quiet and all? Why if jud'st one of my youngins was that quiet, I'd think he'd done gone and run off or got run over or something worse! How old is she?"

Holding up my biscuit filled with syrup in one hand and a Hershey Bar in the other for her to see while dancing from side-to-side in the backseat, I called out, "Hey, Lucy Calhoun, I'm twelve-and-a-half almost."

Unbeknownst to Grandma, Granddaddy had slipped me a Hershey bar after I helped him load some of the grocery bags into the Impala.

"No more questions," she said when she saw my sweet secrets.

"Lucy Calhoun, do you really sing like an angel?" I asked her.

Weber spoke up as if he had been waiting to get in the middle of the conversation. "Maw's singing ain't as good as our cousin Ray Charles' singing is. He is a-coming here real soon because we asked him to come to Goodlife for a spell. Paw don't know it yet. Don't you tell it either 'cause it's a sur-prise. He's a-comin' for Great-Grandma Robinson's one hundredth birthday celebration at Taylor Creek near the wall by the Reynolds' place. Why, we has got dinner on the ground planned. And our cousin Ray is going to sing!"

Hanging half of my body out of the car window while hardly believing the words that had passed through my ears, I cried out, "Oh, go on, Weber. What's that *lie* you're telling?"

"Sweet Jesus, Ma, she don't believe me none, does she?" Weber said, about to cry because I had hurt his feelings.

"Cousin Ray is sure enough a-comin'. I seen his letter with my own eyes," Oprah put in.

Beaming over at his sister, Marvin said, "Oprah can read. She smart."

Oprah smiled back before saying, "I want to change my name one day like my cousin Ray. I want to lose Calhoun like Ray lost Robinson. Then, I want to win a life at a gambling joint for myself so I can help Maw and Paw."

Marvin rolled his eyes at Oprah when she frogged his arm.

"Pray tell," Grandma said.

"He's not a-pullin' your leg none, Myra. We got a letter in the mail last year that Ray was in Los Angeles, California, with his manager, Mister Joe Adams, cuttin' a record called *Born to Lose*. They promised that they'd head on down to Goodlife come the first Saturday in June for Great Grandma's big day. He promised. Hey, would you all like to come? Why, we'd be most happy to have you. That is, if you don't mind being the only white folks there," Lucy offered.

"Oh, please, Granddaddy! Could we? I will do all my Saturday chores on Friday. Can we go?" I begged with my fingers crossed under my left arm for luck.

Granddaddy looked over to Grandma, and she purred like a baby kitten whose momma was moving him out of the rain into a new dry home.

"Sure, Lover Girl. We will go over to the big celebration—that is, if they'll have us," he said, waiting for Lucy Calhoun to back out of her invitation. But she didn't. And I knew right then and there that the Lord God had gotten wind of my letter. I was about to jump out of the car and kiss little Weber or Lucy Calhoun or any one of those five children, but I got hold of myself and scooted on out the car window a little more and turned my face up towards the Mississippi blue sky above and shouted while all the Calhoun children cheered along with me, "Lord, I'm a-coming home! I mean, Ray Charles is a-coming to my new home in Goodlife!"

APPROACHING MAGNOLIA SUNDAY, we soon saw Jack and Jill,

Granddaddy's beloved pair of white-faced collies were waiting about a quarter of a mile from the house. They looked like they owned the whole road. When they caught sight of the Impala, they cut loose and began to run alongside the car like two white streaks of lightning barking and wagging their tails because they hadn't seen a soul all day. Granddaddy would soon reward them with some Pepsi-Cola and ice like always.

The chickens and bantams were roosting in their favorite tree in the front yard. When they heard Jack and Jill carrying on so, they woke up and threw a fit of their own, squawking and screaming like they'd seen a chicken snake or something. We ignored the whole bunch and unloaded the Impala. It was already dusk, and the sun was fading away into the western sky. Soon the lightning bugs would be providing us with a dab light.

"Come on in here and help me put up these groceries and get ready for bed. It's almost seven o'clock," Grandma shouted to me while I was shooing her bantams back up their tree to roost.

"Yes, Ma'am. I'm on my way," I said.

We were all in bed by eight o'clock. As I lay awake in bed, I thought my Saturday had been one of the most wonderful days I had had since I first seen my grandfolks' love for one another when they came for me at the Opportunity House in Goshen. Too, I had a very special feeling. A feeling you only get when *you know that you know* somebody cares about you after I'd written my letter.

THE NEXT WEEK FLEW BY as fast as summer does when you're young, and it was Saturday before we knew it. Grandma Reatha was fixing some covered dishes to carry with us to Great Grandma Robinson's 100th birthday dinner. She made a homemade chicken pie, with plenty of eggs, a pan full of apple and peach fritters, and an egg custard.

I didn't care if I had a bite all day long because I knew this was going to be one of the best days of my life. Food was the last thing on my mind. I helped Granddaddy Spurgeon get a block of ice from the icebox to carry for the ice water since we didn't have enough cold tea to go around, and not nary a soul in Goodlife, but Ed Reynolds could afford that many cold soft drinks.

I had dreams for myself like Lulu had for Eunice to see a bonafide university. One of them would someday leave Goodlife like George Wilkerson had and maybe even go to a bonafide university myself to find my own purpose in life. Then, when I returned, I'd buy everyone, White or Colored, any cold soft drink they wanted from Old Man

Blue's Corner Store while his talking parrot, Lester, looked on calling out their names and mine while whistling and waving his leg onward at us.

When we drove on pass the cemetery, I waved at the concrete statue of Jesus standing on top of my folks' gravesite, but this time I had a smile on my face instead of a tear in my eye. When we got near Ed Reynolds' place, White Shadow, I saw an arch that was curved in front of the wall that surrounded it with a sign to the very top. It read: *Paradise.*

My Lord in heaven, where in the world are, we?

I had heard some of the worst tales you can imagine about the wall that divided up the land and its workers. Ed Reynolds had had it built back in 1923 to keep "the Coloreds in their place," is what I was told. It was about eight feet high and only the Lord God knew how long it was because it separated the cotton, watermelon and cantaloupe fields, and farmland, along with White Shadow, from the rest of Goodlife. Ed Reynolds had made it clear that *everybody* would be *separate* even if they were hired hands.

It reminded me of the Bible story about the wall around Jericho, an ancient city of Palestine, that Joshua had led the march around until it came tumbling down. According to the Bible, Joshua went on to take Jericho from the Canaanites and destroy it. I guess I had heard that story enough in Sunday School to hope one day maybe enough folks would gather and *march* around not only White Shadow's wall but around any other walls I'd yet to see in the world outside of Goodlife but suspected were there. Walls that divide people from each other and keep people from receiving what is rightfully theirs—equality.

Being an orphan, I knew people thought of me as different. Still, I wasn't sure if I had Negro blood flowing through my veins. Somehow that didn't matter to me anymore. Though when I walked the streets of Goodlife and Soso, I could feel folk's eyes on me.

Staying only a hair shy of the wall's fold near White Shadow, it seemed most Colored folks were willing to let well enough alone and tried to turn the other cheek and ignore being mistreated.

Suddenly a great rush of wind hit me while sitting in the Impala and looking across White Shadow's land, and when with my very own two eyes I saw the most beautiful sight a body could ever hope to see. I saw children singing and dancing to the sound of a heavenly music under the crepe myrtle and pecan trees along with wild animals. There were squirrels, blue jays by the pair, redbirds, finches, coons, possums, deer, cows, and a lamb.

Everybody was laughing and right in the middle of them was my *hero* Ray Charles playing the most beautiful white piano—the kind you see in books not knowing if it's real or not nor expecting to ever see one like it, let alone hear one played. And he was singing: *Amazing Grace*.

On his right side sat Grandma Robinson in a rocking chair. She was holding a Bible in her hands. The smile on that old Colored woman's tired, black face was as wide as the Piney Woods and as bright as any star you'd ever expect to see.

We got out of the Impala.

We must all be dead.

I expected to see my folks any second but no, we were very much alive. I knew it for sure when my grandfolks took me by the hands and one of them said, "Come, Child, let's go on in."

Is this the *anointing* they talk about?" I asked Granddaddy.

He never answered me. Instead, he smiled.

I don't mind telling you, I was captivated by the power. I knew I was somewhere near Glory. It was almost Heaven, if not one part of it. Once we walked under the arch that read: *Paradise*, I expected to see those pearly gates or streets made of pure gold I had heard about. But all my eyes would let me see on the other side of the stone-cold brick wall was what looked like a picture of enough land for an entire city. It was mighty fine land. Even the grass that carpeted the pasture was the most beautiful emerald green I had ever seen. The yellow, white, and pink azaleas were, amazingly enough, in full bloom. The smell of their funnel-shaped blossoms breezed through the healthy country air like the vapor that rises out of the pot when you make homemade sugar syrup.

Why in the world would Ed Reynolds keep all this to himself?

He had enough to go around once, if not twice, for all the folks in Goodlife and Soso. For one man to keep all this to himself didn't make good sense to me.

I noticed that somebody had cleaned the pasture up because there weren't any cow patties or horse manure to watch for as we walked. I spotted Lucy Calhoun and Weber under a big pecan tree sitting by a man who looked like he'd jumped right out of a moving picture. She motioned for us to come on over and join them.

"Welcome friends," Lucy said.

Little Weber smiled and made a funny face that said, "I told you so, Miss Myra Boone."

I gave them a wave.

"This is Mister Joe Adams. He is Ray's manager from California.

This is Reatha and Spurgeon Davis and Miss Myra Boone, my neighbors from Goodlife."

When Joe Adams stood up to shake our hands, I knew it was my chance, so I went for it. Without even thinking first, I said, "Hello, Sir. My name is Myra Boone. I was born in Philadelphia, Mississippi. My momma and daddy were killed in a tragic house fire while we were living in Meridian. My daddy knew Ray Charles in Florida when he was a Robinson. They were in a charity home together. Mister Adams, my momma used to sing to me the song *You Are My Sunshine*—the same song Ray Charles sings on the box radio. Do you suppose I could meet him and ask him to sing a song for me? I'd be much appreciative until the day I die if I can. And I promise I won't hurt him."

"I don't see why not," Mister Joe Adams said then laughed and added, "Since you put it *that* way." He got up and took me by the hand and led me over to Ray Charles.

First, we stopped at Great Grandma Robinson's rocking chair. She showed us her large print Bible and said, "I'll admit, I've worn out three Bibles. Today it was Ray who brought me this one for my hundredth birthday. I can see it much better. Special ordered from England. Blessed by Her Majesty the Queen and King James. Yes, my large print Bible flew over with Ray on an airplane all the way from

California. Now I go to church every Sunday. Unless it is raining or snowing, I go," she said with pride while she sat there rocking like she was sitting on the top of a mountain waiting for some preacher man to tell her what page to turn to holding tight to her piece of heaven.

I asked, "Lady, what made you live for a hundred years?"

Reaching out her cracked Colored right hand to stroke my cheek, she told me, "I've had all sorts of complaints, and even diseases, but we grew all our food, except for coffee and flour. I believe that is what kept us healthy—and the good Lord, of course. Little girl, believe it or not, I had it tough, but I've enjoyed life so much!"

I took Great Grandma Robinson's right hand and kissed it before I knew it. I thought she was probably the oldest person I would ever see in my entire life, so I needed to pay my respect and show her that she was loved on her birthday. She nodded and gave me a sweet, honey-filled smile. "Little girl, there are many hidden secrets of the heart, good and evil, amongst us. But you must believe in yourself or else your life's journey will be wasted, and you'll grow old and be alone with yourself. Nobody will care for you. And worst of all, you won't care for yourself either."

I listened.

Mister Adams walked over to the glistening piano and whispered something to Ray Charles. He took him by the hand and walked over our way, and he *gave him to me!* I had never felt such gentleness in my entire life like I felt when Ray Charles took my hands and asked, "Child, what can I do for you?"

While I told Ray my story, he began to sing *You Are My Sunshine* slowly and without any music.

Ray bent down and kissed me on the side of the face, all the time never turning loose of my ugly, scarred hands before he asked, "What are you going to be when you grow up? Do you know your *calling* yet?"

"Why, no. I can't sing, that's for sure. About all I've ever done is write the Lord a letter, but He answered it," I told him and hugged his slim body with my eyes closed. I dared hope that when I opened them, he would be my daddy, but not so.

Looking up, I saw that Ray Charles' face was glowing. I looked around to see if Grandma and Granddaddy Davis had seen Ray Charles sing to me, but all I saw was little Weber Calhoun standing by himself near the edge of Taylor Creek eating one of those apple fritters with a look on his face like a bumblebee feasting on a honeysuckle's rich nectar at the beginning of spring.

Ray Charles let go of my right hand to adjust his dark glasses.

Then he asked, "Why not be a *writer*? What better way to ask the world to *see* than by writing?"

I thought about the faces I had seen many times as I'd walked up-and-down the streets of Ellisville then through the Piney Woods of Soso, Goodlife, Goshen, and Glossolalia that were all on the *outside of life*. I stopped thinking and let my eyes wander *freely* about the crowd of those selfsame faces who were now on the *inside* of *Paradise*.

And Ray Charles kept on smiling.

DEAR LORD GOD

Chapter 16

June 25, 1962

Dear Lord God,

I love You.

Thank You for all of my many blessings. This hot summer's day, I'm writing this letter to ask You to forgive me for my mistake of mailing my first letter down the vents of the living room gas heater last year in Meridian. The letter that killed my folks, Virgil and Marigold, my Great Aunt Annabelle, and maybe my cat, Kitty Momma.

I would give anything to go back and make it right. I cannot write, let alone tell anybody else, how sorry I am. My scarred and ugly hands will forevermore serve as a reminder to me that I didn't do the right thing and tell the truth to somebody about my mistake before the first frost came. I am so, so, so sorry.

The Author and Ray Charles (Robinson)

When Momma and I used to sing with Ray Charles on the box radio You Are My Sunshine, I felt loved.

Pray tell, who is going to love me now? Who is going to pray for me?

I wish that I hadn't written L-I-F-E on my bonafide Prayer Ticket at the Salem Camp Meeting Halloween night last year. The truth is that I didn't have the faith to ask You for Daddy's hearing to be restored any more than when I met Ray Charles to ask You for his blind eyes to be opened.

Romans 8:28 says: "'And we know that all things work together for good to them that love God, to them who are called according to his purpose.'"

Lord God, please open my understanding how this verse fits into my life. Help me to accept Your forgiveness, to forgive and believe in myself so I can go back to school and learn, and to listen like Paula at the Opportunity House told me to do. I need Your help in learning how to forgive others, even though they may never ask for forgiveness like the preacher man at the Salem Camp Meeting, the gang of white boys who egged us, my folks for not knowing they hurt me, and the four boys at Needles School who threw me into the silver garbage can.

I will give this letter to my grandfolks to read. I don't want to hurt them anymore by telling them what I did. I'd rather You work this out for my good as they read it, if You don't mind.

June is almost over, and Needles School will soon begin. I still have the handful of the garden myrrh seeds Paula slipped into my pocket at the Opportunity House for chewing when I feel afraid. I can use them, if need be, though I'd rather write to You. I believe that my hopes and dreams of going to school and learning how to be a bonafide writer may now come true come August.

Love,

Mary "Myra" Boone

Magnolia Sunday, Goodlife, Mississippi, 39437

P.S. And, Lord, please bless everybody that ever said, "Pray for me."

A study guide that suggests a plausible, actionable way to reach the institutional and library market AND foreign markets in both English and translation. A Human Geography course can be crafted around ***Goodlife, Mississippi*** to teach students about the source of place—names and local dialects and the anthropology of place—in other words, *What Made Mississippi: Mississippi.*

Myra Boone and the Varieties of Spiritual Experiences in Goodlife, Mississippi

Goodlife, Mississippi, (Eileen Saint Lauren, ©2022) a novel based on the emergence of authentic faith in its heroine, Mary "Myra" Boone, offers a rich, intellectually bracing platform to help students understand—in a direct, visceral way—three masterworks of theology which appear in the liberal arts catalogues of major colleges and universities:

- **William James –*The Varieties of Religious Experiences: A Study in Human Nature*** (1902)
- **Rudolph Otto –*The Idea of the Holy*** (1917)
- **Mircea Eliade –*The Sacred & the Profane*** (1957)

In this light, ***Goodlife, Mississippi*** delivers a framework for course-length introductions to modern theology. In pairing readings by James, Eliade and Otto with the text of Saint Lauren's richly textured fiction, students will learn and apply the opposing skills of *exegesis* and *eisegesis* to their reading of Saint Lauren's novel and these theological classics. For students enrolled in Spiritual Studies or seminary curricula, these paired readings will strengthen the objective, interpretive skills students apply to their readings of Scripture.

Theme: Quest, Struggle and Celebration

In vernacular language reminiscent of Flannery O'Connor, William Faulkner and Charles Spurgeon, ***Goodlife, Mississippi*** explores the elements of quest, struggle, and celebration the child encounters in a quest for meaning—or what Eliade terms the "sacred"—as she moves through a secular life both "profane" and grotesque. In other words, she must experience ungodly events and survive outrageous events to grasp the significance of her fellow-characters, from the five orphaned girls she meets in "The Opportunity House" (who represent certain Saints and Disciples) to Paula (who is the confident, reassuring embodiment of Saint Paul) to their overseer, Moloch, the Devil incarnate (John Milton and William Shakespeare).

Structure: Sacred Space, Time, Nature, and Self

An introductory theology course based on Saint Lauren's fantastic magical realism will focus on the rudiments of spiritual study this writer evokes with depth and intensity. They are: sacred space, time, nature and self.

Sacred Space

In sacred spaces such as the City of Goodlife or Enoch's Glass House, (book two) Myra experiences a taste, then a full serving, of Heaven. As she passes through the fire of her family's burning house, she glimpses first purgatory then hell, yet emerges with new life. In a more profound way, and guided by Eliade's evocative account of biblical time, Myra's journey represents the concept of the *eternal return,* the endless process by which the seeker abandons with childlike innocence her path to the sacred, but still returns to the road and reaches her holy destination. It represents, perhaps, a path to the physical church.

Sacred Time

It is at this point, Otto's concept of the Holy, the *Mysterium*

Tremendum, the awe, relief, and revelation the seeker feels as she arrives Home—intervenes. As Otto writes: "[this] gentle tide pervades the mind with the deep tranquility of worship." At this juncture, the instructor might ask: Is the seeker's arrival in Heaven temporary or permanent? Is she doomed to repeat the sequence—as some Eastern faiths suggest—or has she actually *returned*? Christianity espouses the return without repetition. It is one reason why the faith relies deeply—as Myra does—on locales (such as Goodlife—a symbol of the new Jerusalem) on physical space (such as the Union Community Church—symbolic of the Duke Chapel and / or the Canterbury Cathedral) and on objects the piece of Cross wood and the Ark of the Covenant—book two— (ranging from relics of the True Cross to rosaries and medallions.)

It is noteworthy that Myra's picaresque journey is non-linear. Her travels are described without a predictable chronology. This suggests that the seeker's quest—though the lens of consciousness—relies on an internal, spiritual clock. By focusing at intervals on *sacred time*, Myra lives within the Near Eastern, even Judaic, realm of the Sacred.

Myra is a wanderer, or nomad, just as the People of the Pentateuch were. Their *40 years* had supernatural significance and their *Sabbath* became the fulcrum of survival. In their harsh and transient world, there were few structures beyond the pyramids in which travelers could find shelter. Indeed, the Ark of the Covenant seems dwarfed by the vast space over which it travelled just as it is in the setting of ***Goodlife, Mississippi*** and found in book two.

In Myra's life, we also experience the significance of Eliade's temporal concepts of *cosmos and chaos*, so crucial to an understanding of Genesis 1 and 2, and to the repeated ways in which the Old Testament God generated order from chaos. In the spirit of Genesis, Myra, the seeker is also a creator. She surmounts and transforms her disabilities into strength, obstacles into pathways, doubts into faith.

Sacred Nature

Saint Lauren's text explodes with natural imagery. There are symbolic breezes stirring the treetops, inner tempest storms that rock the reader's foundations, bursts of fire in Merrihope, family members that give up the Ghost into the starlit sky, and sun-rings encircle a character's head in Goodlife. Characters anoint one another with olive oil, and whales and prophets on stain glassed windows. Flies speak words of darkness, and the Piney Woods offer holy solace and shelter. The sun rises and the moon sets at conspicuous times. Water exercises its magic and the great sky—azure dome or pitch black—is ever-present.

In this way, ***Goodlife, Mississippi*** invokes the *hierophany* (holy, sacred) of nature as Eliade defines it, a universe packed with myriad signs and symbols. In the Saint Lauren's work, natural phenomena are characters which appall, invite, warn, destroy, and shelter both seekers and spiritual predators.

In the author's vivid descriptions of natural phenomena, from emesis to rain, she envisions a world of volcanic meaning. In James' model of spiritual experience, worship cannot occur without sensory experience, whether one finds holiness in the incense of a processional or the solitude and fragrance of wild places. Using exegetical skills, students will learn to discern the holy as Myra does, where she does, *as she does.*

Sacred Self

Myra's deformed body is eventually transformed. Myra seems always to be the *unformed* child on the edge of adolescence, a period in of *initiation* in both James and Eliade's work.

In this light, John Durham, notes in notes on Eliade's *The Sacred & Profane 4* at <Bytrentsacred.co.uk> "…Initiation rites imparted three kinds of *revelation*: about the sacred, about death and about sexuality. They [subjected] initiates to some kind of symbolic death followed by rebirth as a new person."

The Sacred Self is Myra's destination. While her arrival may seem anti-climactic to some readers, Saint Lauren depicts the emergence of the Sacred Self as a life-long process. In order to achieve rebirth, death in all its forms is a prerequisite, and Myra approaches spiritual death at intervals throughout this sequence of picaresque story telling.

Myra Boone and the Varieties and Spiritual Experience in Goodlife, Mississippi

In Jamesian terms, Myra Boone is a "spiritual genius" armed by Eliade's Creator to conquer any dragons which block her from recognition, or revelation, of the "Holy." In Jamesian terms, Myra has "mystical consciousness" and indeed, Saint Lauren's narrative voice is instilled in Myra's, a character who succumbs to spiritual trances and awakens to mystical, transcendent experience repeatedly.

Again, in Jamesian terms, Myra's stories take the divided self with which she begins her tale and reconciles the dichotomy through rebirth and revelation. Had James read Saint Lauren's manuscript, his final question would be whether Myra's rebirth—or second awakening—was enough. Should we expect yet another rebirth?

It is fitting, then, in tribute to Saint Lauren's work and James' deeply pragmatic nature that we quote James' general philosophical position on God's existence as follows:

> "I have no hypotheses to offer beyond what the phenomenon of 'prayerful communion' ... suggests ... The only thing that it unequivocally testifies to is that we can experience union with *something* larger than ourselves and that, in that union, we find our greatest peace."

The synonym of grace to "peace" can be applied to maintain this deeply emotional work to help illuminate the rudiments of active spirituality.

FORTHCOMING BY THE AUTHOR

Eileen Saint Lauren's, MY NEIGHBORS, a collection of short stories set in Goodlife, Mississippi, will be published in 2023.